SAINT NICK

ALSO BY BRADLEY WRIGHT

Xander King Series:

Whiskey & Roses

Vanquish

King's Ransom

King's Reign

Scourge

Vendetta (prequel novella)

Lawson Raines Series:

When the Man Comes Around

Shooting Star

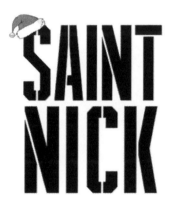

Bradley Wright/King's Ransom Books
www.bradleywrightauthor.com

Publisher's Note: This is a work of fiction. Names, characters, places, and
incidents are a product of the author's imagination. Locales and public
names are sometimes used for atmospheric purposes. Any resemblance to
actual people, living or dead,
or to businesses, companies, events, institutions, or locales is completely
coincidental.

SAINT NICK/Bradley Wright. -- 1st ed.
ISBN - 9781707895984

For my Mom
Of the millions of things you've done right over the years,
Christmas is always at the top of the list. Thanks for ALWAYS
making it fun.
I love you.

Christmas magic is silent. You don't hear it - You feel it. You know it. You believe it.

— KEVIN ALAN MILNE

Christmas is a time when everybody wants his past forgotten and his present remembered.

— PHYLLIS DILLER

SAINT NICK

PROLOGUE

Undisclosed isolated location deep in the desert of Iraq
December 24th, 2018

ARMY RANGER NICK CAMPOS SLAMMED THE NINE AND TEN OF
spades down on the table so hard the poker chips scattered
from their neat little stacks. He'd made his flush on fourth
street, and check-raised his drunken bunk mates until they
gave up nearly all of their money. No one loved a good
bourbon more than Nick, but when he sat down with these
boys to play cards, he only *acted* like he was going drink for
drink with them.

Compared to Nick, these men were babies. He was only
on this detail with these greenhorns as a punishment, so he
didn't feel bad taking advantage of them for their parent's
money. Someone had to pay for him being there.

"Damn, old man." The kid to his left scooted quickly
away from the overturned cup that was spilling his beer
onto the ground. "Why you gotta shake the table?"

Old man. He'd heard that a lot over the last couple days. Though he was only forty, he supposed he was ancient to these new recruits. Spending his days with these pukes was embarrassing enough seeing as how he was maybe the most decorated Army Ranger in history. What made it worse was that they knew he was on thin ice and couldn't clap back at them when they smarted off. One more incident and he was gone, so Nick was forced to play nice.

Nick had smoked his Cuban Cohiba down to the nub, so he raked his chips, ashed it, and stood.

Nick looked at everyone at the table, then pointed to his ever-mounting stack of chips. "I counted these."

He walked away from the table and out through the opening in the tent. Without the fans that were blowing inside, the ninety-degree midnight air was like stepping into an oven. *Merry f'n Christmas.* He'd been in that godforsaken hell hole for half his life, or some other desert just like it. A lot of his fellow Rangers had asked him why he was still there. The words of his commander still rang in his ear.

"Why the hell are you still doing this, Nick? You've got nothing to prove. Don't let you getting court-martialed be the way you leave the Army. Go out the way a hero like you should. Not with all these extracurricular activities. It's time to hang it up."

The latest extracurricular activity in question his commander was speaking of was distributing illegal cigars to himself and some of his fellow Rangers. In and of itself the cigars wouldn't have been a big deal. The commander would normally have looked the other way, but seeing as how an Army-issued vehicle got blown up, and three Iraqis were injured, Nick could see that the commander didn't really have a choice but to dole out some sort of punishment. But after all that Nick had given for his country, he felt like this assignment to train these teenagers on basic weapons tactics was a low blow.

Nick walked out of tent range, unzipped, and began to relieve himself. The commander said it wasn't just about this incident, but the string of them over the last few weeks. So what? Nick beat up a Marine that was running his mouth. Everybody had agreed the douchebag deserved it. And so what, Nick had spread a little cheer with a night of specially procured booze and some ladies. He'd done it for his men. For morale. That alone should have been met with a little bit of grace.

The fact was, Nick knew he was on his last leg as one of the elites. Most men didn't make it past thirty-five at his level of combat and training. But what else was Nick going to do? Go back to Kentucky and sell insurance? Open a gun range and toil away in boredom for the rest of his life? Find a woman and settle down? None of those things were remotely appealing after the adrenaline rush of covert combat operations. And no matter what the commander or any of the rest of the higher-ups thought, Nick knew he still had plenty to give.

Nick zipped his pants and turned back toward the tent. The last thing he wanted to do was go back in there and sit at the table with those boys. Well, sit at the table with them sober at least. He pulled the silver flask his best friend in the world had given him the night before he stepped on an IED and took a long swig of the sweet brown liquor it held.

As he tipped the bottom of the flask toward the sky, something strange up in the clouds at his three o' clock caught his eye. It was like a mist of purple and green in the atmosphere lit up the darkness. He twisted the cap closed to pocket the flask, and that was when he swore he saw something fly right through it. He swallowed hard, and the burn of the bourbon caught in his throat.

"The hell was that?" he said aloud in between coughs.

Nick didn't hear any air-raid sirens. In fact, he didn't hear anything at all. If there was something flying above them that wasn't supposed to be, there would have already been a flurry of commotion. But he knew he saw something come through that mist. The last thing he was going to do was take any chances. He had to go check it out. But he couldn't alert anyone. Not yet. He had been drinking. If he spun everyone up about something flying through the air and then there happened to be nothing, that dishonorable discharge would come down like a hammer.

Nick stalked over to the foot of one of the sand dunes on his right. The Army had positioned this pop-up training spot inside a circle of dunes to keep it a bit more private. Nick bear-crawled his way up to the top and peered out over the dark desert that stretched out in front of him. There was no fire from a crash. From the trajectory it had definitely seemed to be heading toward the ground. But there was no downed aircraft burning in the distance. It would have been impossible to miss in the complete blackness in front of him. He must have just been seeing things after all, and he was glad he hadn't jumped to ring any alarms.

Nick looked back up at the spot in the sky where he thought he'd seen something, shook his head, then turned back toward the tents. Just before he took his first step, the faintest of sounds made it to his ear. He stopped, pricked his ears, and listened intently to the silence in the air.

First, he heard a muffled rumble of laughs from the poker tent. He turned back toward the open desert and leaned in. Then he heard it again.

"Is that . . . bells?"

As absurd as his own words sounded to him out in the middle of terrorist territory, he had no idea what else it could be. Because it sounded exactly like jingling bells.

That's when he heard something clearing its nose with a snort, and what sounded like an animal grunting. Was it . . . a camel?

Nick didn't like the feeling he was getting that *something* was out there. "What the hell's going on?"

Nick pulled his Beretta from his hip holster and moved down the side of the dune that faced the open desert. He had a small flashlight in his cargo pocket, but just in case whatever was out there had ill-intent, he didn't want to alert it of his presence. He tromped his way through the thick sand beneath his boots, keeping his eyes, and his gun, focused on the darkness in front of him.

Nick heard a grunt again, but this one was unmistakably human. It sounded like someone in pain. He picked up his pace a bit, and when the jingling sound came again, there was no mistaking it––it was indeed bells. More animal noises followed, and now that he was closer, they didn't sound as much like the camels that populated the area. They sounded more like the deer he used to hunt back home.

It was so dark that Nick didn't have a choice but to go for his flashlight. He hadn't heard any sounds that would make him think he was in danger. Just the oddest combination of noises he had ever heard in his life. Especially out in the middle of the desert. He flicked the switch, and his beam of light pointed straight down at the sand. His pace slowed as he raised his flashlight. He was resting his Beretta atop his left wrist as he searched the sand.

The moans of pain began again. This time it was clear someone was really in trouble.

Nick didn't call out, just on the off chance this was some sort of weird trap. He wasn't going to give away his position unnecessarily. Though he was the only source of light for miles, other than the Army barracks behind the dunes, which probably made it irrelevant.

The grunts and snorts of multiple animals were just a few steps away now.

"Oh . . . Please!" A long moan of pain followed a man's cry. "Someone!"

Nick's flashlight finally found something other than sand. He searched what was in his beam for a moment, because he couldn't believe his eyes. It was large and red, and it was sitting on . . . skis?

The man's moan became dire––much louder and more frantic. Nick ran around to the other side of what looked like some sort of sled turned on its side. That was when he finally found the source of the moans. There, in his narrow beam of light, clutching at his chest and writhing in the sand, was a man dressed like Santa Claus.

Santa Claus?

"Is this some sort of sick joke?" Nick said to the man lying in the sand.

The only way the man could answer was with a moan of pain.

Nick took the handle of the flashlight in his teeth, holstered his gun, and took a knee beside the man. His face was as red as the dumb costume he was wearing, and it was clear something was really wrong with him. Nick stood, pushed on the sled until it was back upright on its runners, then grabbed the man and hoisted him back into the sled's seat. Nick had to give it to the guy, he was dedicated to the craft, because not only did he look like Santa, he must have eaten like him too. He had to at least be around two-hundred and fifty pounds.

Nick took the flashlight from his mouth and propped it on the rail beside him so he could see the man's face. "All right, take a couple deep breaths," Nick said. "In through the nose, out through the mouth."

The man put both hands on Nick's shoulders and pulled him close. There was desperation in his eyes. "There's no time, Nick. I'm not going to make it."

Nick pulled back, his mouth gaped, and a weird feeling pulsed through his senses. "Nick? How the hell did you know my name?"

"There's no time!" the man shouted through an obviously tremendous amount of pain. His face was scrunched in agony behind his long white beard, and fluffy white eyebrows. "Just listen to me!"

"Look, let me go get my medic. I'll be back with him in ten minutes."

Every word was a struggle for the pained man. "I don't have ten minutes. But what I have is something that I must pass on. All you have to do is sit right here, slap the reins down on the rail, and say 'take me home'."

Nick couldn't believe what he was hearing. Had this man gone insane? Was this man hallucinating because he was in the throes of death? Was it Nick who was hallucinating? He had seen this thing come falling from the sky. Now, on Christmas, he'd found this crazy dude dressed as Santa, dying of a heart attack, talking about getting in his sled and saying take me home?

Nick couldn't help himself, and he began to laugh. Hard. Uncontrollable, gut-busting, hands on the knees laughter. The man clutched one last time at his chest, and finally, his head slumped over and he stopped moving. Nick began to clap. "Bravo," he said between laughs. "Bra-VO! If I had any pull, you'd get an Oscar. I mean, what an elaborate prank!"

Nick swung his flashlight to the right, and the source of all the animal noises was revealed. Attached to the head of the sled by leather harnesses was an entire line of reindeer. "All right, Commander Thompson, come on out. How the hell did you get reindeer out here in the middle of Iraq?"

Nick was truly amazed.

"And the Santa? Wow! Top notch. It must have cost you a fortune to do all this!"

As Nick shined his light over the double line of reindeer, they just stared back at him like *he* was the crazy one.

"Okay. Come on out. You got me!"

Nick walked back toward the sled. The Santa Claus was still slumped over, really selling it. Nick let his light move to the back row of the sled. "There's even a sack? Wow! No expense spared, no detail left undone! I'm impressed."

He walked over to the sack, which still looked full of presents, and opened it. He reached inside and felt nothing. He reached farther down, but the sack just kept going, even down past where the floor of the sled should be. "Oh, now this is a good trick!"

Too good, actually. It left him feeling a sharp eerie feeling, and he quickly pulled his arm back out of the sack like he'd just reached into a bag full of spiders. It still maintained its shape and looked full. None of it made sense.

"Okay, you got me. I'm tired." He walked over to the Santa and gave him a nudge. "It's over. You're gonna get paid. Now wake up and get the hell out of here before some jihadis come running down the sand and take you back to their cave."

The man didn't move after the nudge. "Hey, I'm done playing. Wake up and get the hell outta here."

This time Nick pushed him on the shoulder, much harder, and the man slumped over onto his side on the seat. Nick stepped up into the sled, bent over him, and felt the man's neck.

Dead.

Nick recoiled and scooted to the middle of the sled.

"What the hell is this shit?" He moved his light over the reindeer again, then swung it back behind him at the bottomless sack. Then back over to the dead Santa. The dead Santa that had known his name.

Nick's first thought was selfish. Whatever this was, he was going to get blamed for this weird dead guy, and this was the way his decorated career in the military was going to end. His second thought was absolutely nuts.

Could this actually be Santa?

"What the hell is wrong with me. I've got to get this cleaned up."

As Nick started to step off the sleigh his hand brushed across the thick leather reins attached to the reindeer. *To the reindeer!*

Nick stopped, squared up with the center of the sled, and took the reins in his hands. The man's words echoed in his mind.

All you have to do is sit right here, slap the reins down on the rail, and say 'take me home'.

Nick lifted the reins and slapped them down on the rail. Some bells jingled and the reindeer grunted and moaned and shifted their stances, but that was it.

"Seriously, what the hell am I doing? I've lost my damn mind."

First, he looked into the darkness around him. Mostly to

make sure he was alone. Then he lifted the reins again and slapped them down harder, but this time he said the words the man told him to say.

"Take me home!"

The reins pulled tight in his hands, and bells jingled as the reindeer began to move. Then the sleigh started to inch forward. Nick's mouth dropped open. These things were actually about to move the sleigh.

As the bells jingled more and more, the sled began to pick up speed. A few seconds later he could feel the hot breeze in his face, and a few seconds after that, he felt the front end of the sled tip upward, pinning him to the back of the seat.

"What the fff . . ."

Then the sound of sliding stopped, but the sled was moving faster than ever. Nick scooted to the far edge of his seat and pointed his flashlight past the floorboard. Not only did he not see sand, he didn't see anything. The sled holding a man dressed like Santa Claus and his bottomless sack, being pulled by reindeer, on Christmas Eve, was now flying through the air. It was actually flying through the air.

Nick put a death grip on the rails.

"Wake up wake up wake up WAKE UP!" he shouted as the sled entered a thick white cloud. His flashlight beam looked like a headlight searching through fog.

"Wake up, Nick! Wake up!" he tried one last time. But as the sled broke through the clouds and the moon lit up the row of flying reindeer dancing through the air in front of him, a very strange feeling washed over him—a sense that the life he'd been leading was over, and it felt as real to him as a bullet to the chest. He knew right then he was never going back to his old life, and he couldn't help but feel as if he had been chosen. That must have been how the jolly old dying man knew his name.

Nick had no idea where the reindeer were taking him, or why he was all of a sudden so confident his life was beginning anew. But he was, and all he could do as he floated high above the ground was just sit back and enjoy the ride. With his gun solidly fixed to his hand, of course.

1

Los Angeles Police Department Jail
Hollywood, California
One Year Later, December 23rd 2019

"Is this some sort of joke?"

Jim Calipari, head of the FBI's Los Angeles division, stood with his hands on his hips, looking at Brooke like she had two heads.

"I don't know what this is all about really," Brooke said. "But I couldn't resist having you here when I talk to him. It's not every day you get to hear a story like this."

Brooke and Jim had been on and off for over a year at that point. This was more about playing a playful prank on him than anything else. Or at least she hoped it was going to end up just a prank because the guy's story surely couldn't be anything serious.

Jim took his hand and brushed over the part in his

sandy-blonde hair. "You know I don't have time for this, Brooke. I have actual cases piling higher every single day."

"No one knows that more than me, Jim." It was Brooke's turn to fiddle with her hair, tucking a blonde flyaway back behind her ear. She was enjoying the fact that Jim was getting worked up. "The pile of cases is one of the main reasons we aren't together. That, and the fact that you're an asshole."

Jim gave her the 'ha, ha' smirk.

"Come on," she said, attempting to lighten the mood. "It's a guy who claims to be Santa Claus. Who also claims to have taken out three people on the FBI's most wanted list. How could I not call you?"

Jim rolled his eyes. "Let me see the file."

Brooke walked over to the table in the interrogation room and handed him the file. She had expected him to laugh when he opened the file. But his gaped mouth and sharp inhale were the opposite of what she was expecting.

"This man is here? Right now?" Jim said, pointing to the picture.

"Yeah, he's here. Why? What's wrong? You look like you've seen a ghost."

"Ghost is a pretty fitting way to put it."

An officer walked in and interrupted further explanation. "He's in the hall, you ready for him?"

Jim looked at Brooke, shook his head in disbelief, then nodded to the officer. "Bring him in."

"Okay, *Santa*. Right this way." The officer laughed as he nodded for Nick to follow him into the interrogation room. Nick hadn't had a lot of experience telling people he was

Santa Claus. It had only been a year since the old man passed on the disease, or whatever it was that gave Nick these weird but increasingly useful abilities. However, at the beginning of this month he had decided to just lean into it. Nick had always been proud of being good at two completely contrasting things: Being a complete hard-ass, but also possessing the ability to know when something was just too funny to pass up.

"Keep laughing, officer," Nick said. "Keep on laughing and your daughter won't get that Moana doll she's been asking for."

The look the officer gave him was the reason why he was leaning into this ridiculous Santa thing. The look was a cross between astonished and fright. And Nick would have been lying if he said he didn't love knowing something he wasn't supposed to know. Especially in a situation like this one where he could disarm the 'tough guy' security guard by knowing exactly what his daughter's been begging for for Christmas.

The officer moved behind Nick and gave him a nudge in the direction of the room.

Nick smiled. "What? Something I said?"

The officer didn't respond. Nick continued forward. He'd been told he was being taken to speak with someone high in the ranks of the FBI. He already knew who they were taking him to see, but when he walked into the room and actually saw Jim Calipari standing on the other side of the table, he couldn't suppress the wide smile that grew across his face. His plan had worked. So far.

"Well, well, well. If it isn't my old boot camp bunk mate," Nick said with his arms spread wide.

The blonde in the room beside Jim shot him a look of disbelief.

Jim waved off the officer behind Nick. "Nick Campos? What the hell are you doing here? And why are you wearing that ridiculous outfit?"

It's not what you think––Nick wasn't wearing a full-on Santa suit. He wasn't going to lean into the character *that* much.

Nick looked down at his hunter-green V-neck tee, camo pants, and black Army boots. What Jim was referring to as 'ridiculous' was the thick white utility belt with the big black buckle strapped around Nick's waist. It had places for two sidearms, two extra magazines, an EDC knife, and even a grenade or two if he was feeling frisky. Of course, from where Jim stood, it just looked like a silly Santa belt that had no place on an otherwise standard issue Army uniform.

"Jack thought it added a nice touch," Nick said.

"It looks ridiculous," Jim said. "And who the hell is Jack?"

"Well, I'm sure by now you've heard that I'm Santa Claus, so this belt can't seem *that* ridiculous. Jack is my head elf."

Even though it was the truth, that admission usually got a laugh. But Jim just shook his head and frowned.

"What the hell are you doing, Nick? You've always been a crazy son of a bitch, but have you finally, completely lost your mind?"

Nick looked over at the woman standing beside Jim. "I look crazy to you?"

"No," she said. "The story is a bit crazy, but you seem fine to me."

"You hear that, Jim? Your girlfriend says I'm fine."

Nick walked forward, pulled out the metal folding chair and took a seat. "Jim, you mind if we skip the thing where we act like we give a damn about each other and get right to the part where I tell you that I was about to take out the fourth most wanted man on your list in a matter of two weeks when the LAPD wrongfully arrested me for assault?"

Jim took a seat opposite Nick and nodded for Brooke to do the same. "You punched an off-duty officer in the face outside of a bar, then took a piss in his beer. You don't think that merits an arrest?"

"Not if you saw the way he was groping that nice young lady just trying to have a drink with her friends."

Jim scoffed. "Oh, so now Nick Campos is a gentleman? You expect me to believe that?"

"Gentleman, vigilante hero, Jolly Old Saint Nick . . . I have a lot of titles these days."

Jim was getting ready to rebut when Brooke spoke up. "Clearly the two of you have a history that I care nothing about. What I do care about is what you said *before* you said you were wrongfully arrested." Brooke looked over at Jim and gave him a cold look. "Which is supposed to be why we were brought down to this jail in the first place—to listen to your seemingly bullshit story about who you are, and why you are taking down FBI-wanted criminals. Can we just get to that? Because some of us have actual criminals to investigate. Not whatever the hell this is."

"Ooh, you've got yourself a pistol here, Jim. I like her. You should have treated her better."

"First of all, Agent Sanders and I are not together—"

"Ah-ah, Jim. Don't forget who you're talking to now," Nick gave a devilish grin. "I see you when you're sleeping. So that means I see who you are sleeping with."

Jim huffed and rose to his feet. "All right, that's enough." He looked to the door. "Officer? Come get this man and take him back to his holding cell."

Nick knew he'd hit a nerve. Now it was time to step on it.

The other thing he loved most about what the fat man in the desert had passed on to him was knowing everything about everyone. It wasn't that Nick could read minds, but he could see all of their actions and knew everything about them, including where they lived.

"Samuel Epstein lives at 4537 Washburn Ave." Nick started in. "Over the last twelve months, he has raped six women, murdered four, and stole a Snickers candy bar from the 7/11 on Sunset. Now, I don't imagine that monster is on your most wanted list for stealing the Snickers bar. So, when I was watching him pick out his next victim at the bar last night, I was going to do your job for you and end the son of bitch. But like I said, I was wrongfully arrested."

Brooke leaned forward. "And the real reason you punched the cop was because you were upset that he let Epstein get away?"

Brooke was half right. Nick looked over at Jim and smiled. "She's the smart one, I see. You really messed things up letting her go."

Jim slammed his fist down on the table. Brooke jumped, and Nick just held his smile. "That is your proof that you're Santa Claus? Because you read the paper about Epstein's crimes and claim to know the address of one of our most wanted? Did you think I was going to bail you out of jail or something? Just because you came up with this whole cockamamie story? So they would call me? What a waste of time. Great to see you, Nick. Hope the next twenty years goes a little better for you."

Nick didn't lose his cool. He looked over at Brooke. "He always this loud? Take it easy, Jim. You're gonna have a heart attack or something."

Jim was seething. He began to pace the room behind Brooke.

While Nick and Jim were going back and forth, Brooke was staying focused. "You told this information about Epstein's address to your arresting officer, didn't you?"

"I did," Nick said. "But I doubt he even wrote it down."

Jim stopped pacing and shot an inquisitive look at Brooke. "No, he wrote it down," she said. "And actually, I just got an email saying they went to check the address out an hour ago and Epstein went running out the back door."

"What?" Jim said. His look morphed from an eyebrow raise to pure shock.

"Yeah. They ran him down and arrested him. Nick's tip led to the arrest of Samuel Epstein."

Jim had no words.

Nick always had something to say.

"Arrest? Great." Nick shook his head. "Now he'll get off on some technicality. Should have just let me handle it."

"Shut the hell up, Nick. Right now." Jim pointed. Then looked back at Brooke. "You're serious?"

"Dead serious. Epstein is in custody as we speak."

"How the hell did you know where he was staying, Nick? You working with him? Ratting on him to keep your-self in the clear?"

"Jim?" Brooke interrupted.

"It's okay, Brooke." Nick stood. "The same way I know where you live, Jim. Same as I know that Brooke Abigail Sanders here lives at 639 Perry Street and the only thing she wants for Christmas is a trip to Hawaii to get the hell away from you for a few days."

Both Jim and Nick looked over at Brooke. Her mouth was literally hanging open. Nick loved it when that happened.

Jim put both his hands on his hips. "This is absurd.

Okay, Santa. Big reveal there. Literally everyone on the planet wants a trip to Hawaii."

"Okay, I can do you if you want."

"He was right about me," Brooke said.

"Sure . . . Fine," Jim said. "What do *I* want for Christmas Mr. Kringle?"

"You sure you want me to say it in front of Brooke?"

"What would that matter? Just get it over with and say it so we can move on."

"Okay . . ." Nick shrugged. "You want Karen Johnson of 3951 Walbash Court to accept your invitation to Christmas dinner. Then you want to pin her legs back behind her—"

"All right, that's it!"

Jim came storming around the table, took two fistfuls of Nick's shirt, and shoved him backward until his back was pinned against the two-way mirror.

Nick didn't acknowledge Jim. Instead, he looked over Jim's shoulder at Brooke. "Remember what I said about knowing who you're sleeping with? Yeah, he's already slept with Karen too. Last week. The night after the last night the two of you were together. What do you see in this guy anyway?"

Jim punched Nick in the stomach. Nick doubled over, but also began to laugh. "It's a pattern, Brooke. For over twenty years it seems."

Jim lifted Nick back up and pinned him back against the mirror by his shoulders. "Shut your mouth!"

"Jimmy here slept with the girl I met during boot camp." Then he looked Jim in the eyes. "Merry Christmas, shit stain."

2

BROOKE, WEARING AN EXPRESSION OF DISGUST, MANAGED TO separate the two of them, and sit them back down in an attempt to resume some sort of civil conversation.

They never got the chance.

Three men in black suits burst through the interrogation room door.

Jim stood. "What the hell are you doing? This is a closed interrogation. You can't be in here. Officer!"

A short man in the same black suit as the other three walked through the door holding his credentials out in front of him. "Well, I'm Special Agent Donald Andrews, and it's my interrogation now."

Unlike Jim, Nick wasn't surprised the CIA was there. Nick had been keeping his eye on the CIA's investigation of an unidentified flying object that had crashed in the desert of Iraq about a year ago. Nick had used Santa's passed-along ability to see everything to find the video on an eleven-year-old boy's digital cloud. Then he enlisted Jack to have his elves to work their magic and enhance the ultra-low-resolution video until reindeer and a sleigh could actually be seen falling from the sky. He then sent the video to the CIA and told them what he wanted to do.

"Why are you here?" Jim said. "What the hell do you know about what's going on here?"

The short and skinny Agent Andrews was smug. It was written all over his face. Nick could tell just by looking that he was a classic case of the Napoleon Complex.

Andrews sniffed like someone who thinks he knows everything would, hiked up his trousers by the belt and smirked. If he'd been wearing an old cop uniform instead of the CIA suit, he would have almost literally been Mayberry's finest, Barney Fife. "Maybe you should ask your old boot camp pal that question. He's been dropping hints for half a year now."

Jim looked over at Nick, and his mouth was slightly agape. Nick couldn't help but smile. When he had decided to try to make his presence known in this manner, Nick never thought it would all work out this perfectly. *Santa really does have some magic.* He figured he would at least be able to break up Jim's relationship with Brooke for good. Outing him as a cheater would easily do that. In studying Brooke from afar, it was clear that she was in no way the type of woman who would stand for that. And even though Nick orchestrated this little meet and greet with the CIA coming in, he never thought he would actually get to watch the CIA strip away what might be the biggest story in US crime fighting history away from Jim. *Serves the son of a bitch right.* Nick had really liked Sarah back in the day before Jim got her drunk and took advantage of her.

"I don't understand," Jim said. He was still looking at Nick with a blank stare as if his processor was broken.

Andrews took the only empty seat left, turned it around backwards and straddled it. "The CIA really didn't know what to make of the video that was anonymously sent to us. I mean, it was Santa and his reindeer falling from the sky. Obviously, we just thought it was a stupid prank."

Nick thought the look on Jim's face was priceless. It had to be a real kick in the nuts for the FBI man to hear the CIA man actually explaining that Santa had crashed his sleigh. If Nick hadn't been there at the crash himself, he would have punched Agent Andrews in the mouth for insulting his intelligence.

"Obviously it was a prank, because it's ridiculous," Jim said.

Nick laughed. "Was ridiculous the word of the day on your toilet paper or something, Jim? 'Cause you sure are wearing it out."

Jim's f-bomb-laden response was exactly what Nick had hoped for.

"Like I was saying," Andrews continued. "We thought it had to be a fake too, until we saw headlines that an Army Ranger disappeared from the face of the Earth in almost the exact same location, on the exact same night."

Jim's head swung toward Nick so fast he must have gotten whiplash.

"I tried to tell you, Jim," Nick said.

Jim couldn't speak.

"So what?" Brooke said. "So a Ranger—Nick—went missing the same night as someone took a prank video of a sleigh in the sky. How does that even remotely correlate to this psycho now being Santa Claus?"

"Psycho?" Nick said. "Somebody must not want that Hawaiian vacation that bad after all."

"Oh shut up, would you?" Brooke stood from her chair. "I've got work to do. *Real* work. I'll let you chase your tail on this nonsense, Agent Andrews. Good luck keeping your job when he turns out to be a total fraud with a complete lack of magical powers."

"1989, you got a Dance Club Barbie."

Brooke stopped in her tracks as she reached the door. "Big deal. Every girl got a Barbie in 1989.

"1990—Gameboy."

"Same," Brooke put her hands on her hips. "Lucky guess on years. Doesn't mean you have special powers."

"Okay, 1992. You didn't get a Christmas present."

Nick watched Brooke closely. He really didn't want to have to say this, but she had forced his hand. Nick saw Jim and Andrews both look at Brooke's face.

"How—how could you . . ." Brooke trailed off. "You don't know what you're talking about." She turned to walk out of the room, but Nick's next remark stopped her cold.

"You didn't get a present that year because dear ole dad wouldn't let you have one. Santa delivered, but he threw it out before you could wake up and see it. For about two months straight your pops was getting drunk every night and taking his aggressions out on you. Your mom was too cowardly to stop it, and your brother was too young. You took the beatings for you and your brother. Everything your brother did to piss your dad off, you took the blame and felt the wrath. This is exactly the reason I couldn't just sit around up there at the North Pole—fat, dumb, and happy— and just keep delivering presents while I ignored shit like this. What kind of man knows this stuff is going on and does nothing about it? Not the kind of Santa I want flying around."

Nick had said too much, and he knew it. Public relations had never been his strong suit.

"Anyway," he softened his tone. "Was that magical-powery enough for you?"

"That's amazing.," Andrews said. Then he looked over at Jim. "When he did this to about six of my superiors, as you can imagine, we knew then he could be a huge asset. The FBI most wanted list was his proof to us he could do it. This whole thing with you was what, Nick? Revenge? Didn't matter to us as long as he joined our team."

Brooke turned around. Nick could tell by the look on her face that she had swallowed a lot of emotion after his little speech about her dad. "This has all been one big show?" She looked Nick dead in the eyes. "You small and petty man. All of this over a girl from twenty years ago? Disgusting."

Brooke turned and stormed out of the room.

"Wait," Nick said. "Wait!"

But Brooke didn't return.

"Go get her," Nick said. "I'm adding one more demand for my services."

Andrews nodded to his men to go get Brooke. "Bring her back in here please."

"Does he work for you, Agent Andrews?" Jim said. "Or do you work for him?"

Andrews gave a Barney Fife laugh. "Jim, he's Santa Claus. Being a CIA agent doesn't pay all that well. He can give me whatever he wants for Christmas. Think I'll just stay on his good side. Sucks for you though."

Jim rolled his eyes and began gathering his things.

Nick couldn't help it. "Ridiculous, right, Jimmy?"

Andrew's men returned with Brooke. She did not look happy. "What? What else could you possibly want from me?"

Everyone looked to Nick.

"I'm in, Agent Andrews. I'll help the CIA keep the country safe. It suits me better than eating cookies and delivering presents. But you said I had to have an agent work alongside me—to make sure I was following the code or whatever the CIA has to go by. Those were your director's demands, right?"

"Right," Andrews confirmed.

Nick looked back at Brooke.

"What?" she said. "Me? Are you kidding? After what you did here?"

"She's not CIA, Nick," Andrews said.

"But being FBI, she knows most of the protocol, and you can bring her up to speed on the rest, right?"

Andrews looked at Brooke, then back to Nick. "Yeah, okay. We can make it work."

"No. *Hell,* no." Brooke tried to leave, but the men in black blocked the door. "I'm not working with you."

"She's not working with him," Jim chimed in.

"No one is asking you, Jim," Andrews said. Then to Nick, "You sure this is what you want? Might be a bit contentious."

"Come on," Nick smiled at Brooke. "I promise. It'll be fun."

"No."

"She works for me, not the CIA," Jim said.

"Go to hell, Jim," Brooke said. Then she looked at Andrews. "Is this really my only choice here?" She pointed at Jim. "Work for the asshole who treated me like dirt," she moved her finger to Nick, "or . . . Santa Claus?"

"Afraid so, ma'am," Andrews said.

Brooke put her hands on her hips. She looked back and forth between the two of them a few times. Then looked at Nick with an expression of disgust. "Okay then, Santa."

"Call me Nick."

"Okay, Nick. I'll babysit you on whatever this little

publicity stunt is, or whatever you're doing." To Andrews, "But I want a raise. And I want that vacation to Hawaii."

"Can't guarantee you how big, but the raise I can do. The vacation to Hawaii is up to the Claus."

Brooke looked at Nick and rolled her eyes.

Nick was satisfied with how all of this had gone down. He was ready to do what he had always done best and protect his country. Theatrics weren't really his thing, but he was glad he'd gone through with all of it. As creepy as it was, as he had watched Brooke to learn about her, so he could pull this little stunt on Jim, there was something he really liked about her. She wasn't model beautiful, but she was a pretty woman. It was more about the way she stood up to Jim. And the way she was passionate about her job. That was sexy. He was happy to have her come along with him. Even if she didn't really want to. Mrs. Claus and the elves were great people, but the North Pole was getting real damn lonely. Some spunk around the village would be nice.

"No Hawaii, no deal. I'll just go to work for my uncle," Brooke said.

Nick was happy to oblige.

"In that case, Brooke . . . aloha."

3

NICK, BROOKE, AGENT ANDREWS, AND HIS MEN IN BLACK ALL walked out into the setting sun. The tangerine sky backlit the palm-lined street. Nick paused for a moment to take it in. Contrary to how magical popular literature made the North Pole seem, there hadn't been a day of sunshine there in months. And with only one sunset the entire year, it made Nick appreciate the shimmery one that was currently coloring the Los Angeles sky. He did his best to ignore the layer of smog rolling over it.

"Certainly didn't take you for sunset man," Brooke said.

Actually, Nick had always appreciated the beauty of sunrise and sunset. He also enjoyed the beauty of a Patriot missile slamming into the side of an enemy aircraft. He considered himself a complicated man.

"Well, you don't know me," Nick said. "So there's that. And just wait," he nodded toward the fiery ball, "the sun won't be coming out for a few months where we're going. Might want to soak this one in."

"We're going to get everything set up on our end, Nick," Agent Andrews interrupted. Then to Brooke, "I'll email you all the pertinent information. It's not much different than you're used to. Just some higher classification stuff, and some guidelines we'll need Nick here to follow."

"So, basically I'm his babysitter?" she said.

"That's the negative way to look at it. But if I were you, I'd think of myself as his handler. Gives you some power back. You ladies are all about that these days, right?"

Apparently the CIA hadn't really taught Andrews much about people relations either.

Brooke didn't dignify it with a response.

"We'll take it from here, Andrews," Nick said.

Andrews put his sunglasses on in such a way that would make any man want to punch him––like someone who thinks he's cool. Being cool is just something you are. Otherwise, you're just trying too hard. And Andrews was trying *way* too hard.

The four agency men got in their cliché black SUV and drove off.

Brooke turned to Nick. She was facing the dying light, and the orange gave a warm glow to her face. She was much better looking in person. Santa's All-Seeing Eye didn't do her justice. "Okay, Nick. Now that there is no one left to put on a show for, what the hell are we doing? And why the hell did you involve me?"

The first answer was a long one, but the second was easy: In a last-minute effort to piss Jim off, Nick had had the idea to make her work with him. Totally spur of the moment. But he wasn't going to tell her that. Or tell her that there was something about her that reminded Nick of himself. Probably her feisty nature.

"It's pretty simple," Nick said. "We're going to catch some bad guys. The *real* bad ones. The guys that are trying to pull things off like 9/11 again. I'm an Army Ranger,

Brooke. It's in my blood. Taking out the three small-time FBI most wanted guys was just to show the CIA what I could do for them."

"Okay, Nick. But why involve me? And you'd better not say it was to piss Jim off."

"It was to piss Jim off."

Nick had changed his mind. He didn't want to start their partnership off with a lie. Nick was a lot of things that weren't great, but a liar wasn't one of them.

Brooke scoffed and rolled her eyes.

"I'm kidding." He wasn't kidding. "Honestly, Agent Barney Fife back there," Brooke couldn't help but chuckle at the comparison, "is making me have an experienced agent with me at all times. I don't need a babysitter. I've been taking down terrorists for years. But if I have to have one, the devil you know is better than the devil you don't."

"I'm the devil in this scenario?" Brooke said.

"Yes."

"But you don't know me."

"True, but what if they stuck me with someone like Andrews?" Nick squinted his eyes and rubbed his stomach to feign that the thought of that made him sick.

"Okay, I'll give you that. But you know I already hate you. I made that pretty clear back inside."

"Also true. But I'm used to women hating me. So this will just be par for the course."

Nick could tell by the blank stare that Brooke was doing her best to decipher just how full of shit he actually was.

Nick started walking down the sidewalk. "Also, I think it'll be good for Mrs. Claus to have another female to talk too. She's a sweet lady, but she's driving me nuts."

"Wait, you're married?"

Nick raised his eyebrow when he turned to face her as

he backpedaled. "Married? No. Mrs. Claus, you know, the fat man's wife."

"I can't believe this is my life right now," Brooke said, shaking her head.

"You think it seems weird now, just wait." Nick laughed as he turned down the alley behind the police station. "This next bit's gonna blow your mind."

"What are we doing in an alley?"

"Flying home, of course."

Brooke looked down the alley. There were no vehicles. Just a few clumps of trash and a dumpster.

"Fly home in what, exactly? You're not going to tell me you can make garbage bins fly now, are you?"

Nick pulled a key fob from his pocket. "Nope. It's much, much crazier than that."

Nick hit the button and watched Brooke's face. When he saw her jaw drop, he knew the sleigh and the eight reindeer behind him had been revealed. Brooke just stood frozen, her eyes wide with astonishment.

"Get used to that feeling. Things don't work at the North Pole the way they do down here. It took me six months for the shock to wear off."

Brooke was still speechless. She raised her arm and pointed behind Nick. "There's a . . . That's a . . . And those are . . ."

"Yeah, a sleigh and some reindeer."

"How did . . ."

"I pushed this button when the officer gave me back my things earlier. Signaled for Jack to bring my ride. It's like Uber for the year 2075."

Brooke began inching closer to the sleigh. One unbelieving step at a time. "Why couldn't I—"

"See it a second ago? Santa's cloaking device. One of the

many wonders you will find at the NP. See why I couldn't just sit around getting diabetes from eating cookies and spoiling children? I'm a soldier. You give me the ability to see what the bad guys are doing and a twenty-second century cloaking device, and I'm going to take 'em down. The only presents I plan on leaving are grenades in these asshole's stockings."

For a moment Brooke broke her trance from the sleigh and eyed Nick. "Who talks like that?"

"An Army Ranger. We're not like guys like Jim. We don't just *talk* about taking bad people down, we actually do it."

"Okay, Ice Man." Brooke went back to looking at the sleigh in bewilderment and walked forward. She ran her hand along the wooden rail at the back of the sleigh. Nick knew that seeing wasn't necessarily believing when a sleigh and reindeer magically appear.

"You can pet the reindeer too. They're real friendly. Vixen gets a little edgy when she hasn't had her food, but overall she's a sweetheart."

Brooke gave him a sidelong look. "You're enjoying this, aren't you?"

"Other than a couple of paper pushers at the CIA, I haven't been able to really tell anyone. It makes it seem more real to me too, now that I can. But to be honest with you, I'm just chomping at the bit—" Nick looked back at the reindeer, "No pun intended guys," then back to Brooke, "I'm ready to use all this stuff for some real good. To keep the country safe. It's the only thing I've ever been good at."

Brooke looked at him in a way he hadn't seen her look at him since he met her. Almost like she didn't loathe him.

"All right," Brooke said. "I guess I'm going to have to just make the most of this until I can get back to my own investigations. I'll get some things in order and we'll get started tomorrow morning."

A small man with a pointed green hat on popped up from the backseat of the sleigh. "I'm sorry, but we have to get going right now."

Brooke gasped and jumped back from the sleigh. "Good god, where the hell did you come from?"

"I've been right here, on the computer. I've been getting everything ready for you."

Nick walked to the back of the sleigh. "Sorry, Jack, this is Brooke. Brooke, this is Jack. He runs the show for Santa Claus."

"Now I run the show for you, Nick. Nice to meet you, Brooke. Now hop in, we've got to go."

"Did I mention he's a little demanding?" Nick smiled.

"You'll appreciate how demanding I am, Nick, when it saves your life," Jack said.

"I see you just get along great with everyone don't you, Nick?" Brooke said. Then to Jack, "Well, Jack, it's nice to meet you, but I have to have my things before I go anywhere. Especially seeing as how I have no idea how long I'll be gone."

"Sorry, no need. We've inventoried your things and can access them at any moment." Jack turned his back on her, then turned around holding the winter coat Brooke kept in the back of her closet. "You'll need this now. It's really cold where we're going. I've got your gloves, scarf, and beanie hat as well."

"How the hell did you get my coat?"

Nick pulled himself up into the sleigh and held out his hand to help Brooke up. "I told you. Things don't work here like they do in the NP . . . Shall we?"

Brooke snatched her coat from Jack, then bypassed

Nick's hand to get in the sleigh herself. Nick just laughed. He knew her foul mood would turn around as soon as they flew over Santa's village. Even Nick, the hardened war veteran, had been reduced to the excitement of a little boy when he saw it the first time. He knew Brooke would be no different.

4

AFTER ONLY A FEW MINUTES IN WHAT COULD ONLY BE classified as something of a fast forward time warp, the sleigh broke through some sort of horizon barrier and went back to real time. Nick was happy to see that it was a clear night over the village. The stars were magically bright, and so too was the moon. He'd been up with the reindeer almost every night for the past six months, getting used to all the controls, and he'd only seen the sky this perfect a couple of times.

"I can't believe this," Brooke said, her face full of wonder as she looked up into the twinkling night. "Where are we?"

"We're here." Nick pointed forward as the reindeer began their descent. In front of her was a small smattering of lights, standing out in the otherwise complete darkness. The closer they became, the more it shaped into a small village.

"Santa's village," Nick said.

For the moment, the hatred of her situation disappeared, and Brooke was swept away entirely with wonder. The first time Nick saw it a year ago, after being whisked from the desert, it had blown his mind too. However, dealing with a dead Santa and the hysterical Mrs. Claus when he landed that night had been a bit of a buzz kill.

The next couple of months after that were a very strange time for Nick. He was used to being around strangers—twenty years in the Army and that was how a lot of your time was spent—but, at first, everyone at the North Pole hated Nick. They blamed him for the death of the man they loved more than anything else. Nick showing up had been like a bad dream for them—their worst nightmare come true.

It was contentious on both sides. Nick wanted no part of the fat man's business. The only time he'd ever even been around a kid was when he rescued some refugees just outside of Baghdad. He'd had to carry a young boy for over three miles, and he swore to himself then that he would never have one of those smelly life-suckers. So he sure as hell didn't give a damn about taking presents to all the spoiled little brats around the world. The elves resented him for that too.

After a period of mourning, Mrs. Claus was the only one that took to Nick. She said she understood him, because apparently they had kids and one of the boys, Fred, was a real black sheep. Nick hadn't met Fred, but Joseph, their other son, was the spitting image of heart-attack-Santa. Joseph wasn't real happy about dear ole dad passing along the powers to Nick, but he understood the circumstances. Mrs. Claus and Joseph helped the elves understand that Nick hadn't chosen the situation either—that the situation had chosen him. It sounded good to the elves, but Nick hated it. All he wanted to do was get back to his life of duty to his country, so for a while, he was miserable not being able to fight.

It wasn't until he stumbled across Santa's little shooting range that a plan began to form in his mind. The day he'd gone and spent about a thousand rounds on the range, then went back and tinkered with the All-Seeing Eye, everything changed. He knew that with Santa's tools, he could do more good in a week than he could do in a lifetime as a Ranger. The hard part would be getting the US government to play along. Now, here he was, the power of the United States at his back, and an entirely unbelievable set of abilities in front of him.

The last six months of his time at the NP had been spent getting ready for that very day. And after a year of lost time, he was ready to get back into action.

"This—this can't be real," Brooke said. Her eyes still full of wonder.

The sleigh coasted down onto a long pillow of snow, right in the middle of the village. The buildings that surrounded them were all of traditional Nordic architecture. The criss-crossing timber framing ran along the outer walls, giving you the feeling you were in a quaint Danish town. Each of the buildings was covered in tiny yellow lights, the glow of which gave the entire village a warm feeling, even though temperatures were always below zero in the winter.

The reindeer pulled to a stop, right at the feet of a large woman and a crowd of little people. The woman walked over and greeted Brooke with a bear hug.

"Brooke, this is Mrs. Claus," Nick said as he stepped off the sleigh behind her.

As soon as Mrs. Claus said hello, she immediately moved to Nick. "Where have you been? I was so worried."

Nick could feel the motherly presence. In one way it was nice to have someone care about him. He had grown close to her over the past year. On the other hand, he was a forty-year-old man. He didn't need to check in with Santa Claus's wife.

Before Nick could answer, someone was shouting his name.

"Nick, come quick!"

A little man dressed mostly like an elf came running around the corner of Workshop A (yep, there was really a Santa's workshop––many of them). Zeke was only *mostly* dressed like an elf because he only halfway followed their dress protocol. He wore the green elf pants and shirt, but he had on a pair of vintage Air Jordans instead of elf boots, and instead of a clean shaven face and groomed hair, he sported a Fu Manchu mustache, and his long, flowing hair was pulled back into a ponytail. Zeke had been banned from the assembly lines because all he wanted to do was make every toy into a weapon. He was so good at it that he blew up Workshop D back in March. Ever since then, Nick had taken him under his wing. Since they both were *outcasts*, and Zeke loved weapons, Nick found a lot in common with him. The other side of Zeke—the completely batshit crazy side—Nick just decided he would deal with. Because the little dude was seriously a genius when it came to weaponry, and he was fearless. Nick had kept him busy for a while now, and some of the things he'd built were down-right astonishing.

Zeke ran up to Nick, his chest was heaving, and he could hardly form words. "You have to follow me, boss. Like, right now."

This wasn't the first time Zeke had come running in a panic. The first time was at three in the morning. He'd busted into Nick's room and came an arm hair from eating a bullet. All to find out he had simply doubled the power of a hand grenade without having to change the size. Great info, but it could have waited till morning. Ever since then Nick has been trying to talk him down from several bouts of overexcitement. Apparently it still hadn't sunk in.

"I'm busy right now, Z," Nick said. "I need to show Brooke around."

"No! You have to come now!"

Mrs. Claus rolled her eyes and mumbled something as she stepped away.

"Z, seriously, you have got to—"

"It's an American agent! He's about to walk into an ambush!"

Nick had no idea what Zeke was talking about. He *had* been pretty preoccupied the past week putting on a show for the CIA. But, it didn't really matter, because however Zeke had come across this information about an American agent in trouble—if it was actually true—Nick wasn't going to let something happen to an American agent if he could do something to stop it.

5

AFTER THE FOUR-BLOCK RUN, ZEKE THREW THE DOOR OPEN TO Workshop Z. Z was where the misfits did their work. Far away from the toymakers, so Zeke couldn't blow anyone else up if he made a misstep with one of his weapons. Zeke liked it because his name started with a Z. Nick liked it because it was a safe distance from that god-awful Christmas music all the other workshops had on loop. *All* year round.

Nick flipped on the light. The workshop lit up, and what looked like Iron Man's basement appeared. Brooke had come along with Zeke and Nick, and he heard her gasp when she saw Zeke's creations. It was probably the two armor-plated Santa suits right in front of them that made her take pause. They were the part of the warehouse that made it look like Iron Man's basement, because the suits were made of Nitinol, just like the one Iron Man wore in the movies. It didn't have rocket boosters that could help Nick fly, but don't think Zeke wasn't working on it. The other difference was that it didn't have a helmet. But the suit itself was a shimmering crimson, formed for Nick's body, and had a few gadgets that, so far, had tested well. The idea for it had come from one of Nick and Zeke's first nights together after Zeke blew up the workshop. Nick brought out some bourbon, and after quite a few, Iron Man came on television and Zeke swore he could replicate the suit. Nick dared him to try, and a few months later there was actually a working prototype. People had no idea the capacity of these elves. Wooden horses and baby-dolls were things of the past. They could almost build a rocket ship at this point.

"What the hell is that?" Brooke pointed to some more sets of Nitinol armor with four legs instead of two.

Nick was getting ready to tell her they were Iron Man suits for the reindeer, but Zeke interrupted.

"We don't have time for this, boss! Come look!"

On the far right side of the warehouse, there was what Zeke called his war room. A dozen screens wired into a whole lot of things that Nick didn't understand without a PhD in electrical engineering. Most importantly, the main screen in the middle was wired into one thing he would never understand: The All-Seeing Eye. Or the ASE as the elves unimaginatively called it. Zeke ran up to it, plopped down in his chair, and began banging away on the keyboard. A few seconds later, images of a man in a black trench coat sidling up to a wall came into view. It was dark where the man was, but the ASE showed him almost as if the sun was out. A slight green hue was the only difference between night and day.

"What am I looking at, Zeke?"

"Special Agent Justin Kimber. He's just outside of London."

"How do you know this?" Nick said.

"Earlier today, I was doing what you said and was just playing around with the list of trade keywords that your

Agent Andrews sent us. I tried the first combination of words he had listed, *agent, target,* and *eliminate,* and set up an alert if that combination was used in one conversation. As I was working on the hand rockets for your suit just a few minutes ago, I got a ping on those keywords and the ASE took me here."

"What the hell am I looking at?" Brooke said.

"This is the ASE. It's how Santa knows if you've been naughty or nice," Nick said.

Nick looked over and Brooke looked dumbfounded.

"You're serious?" Brooke said.

"As a heart attack."

Zeke cringed and looked back over his shoulder. "Poor choice of words, boss."

"Yeah, sorry." Everyone in the village was still stinging over the way Santa had died.

"So you can really see anyone at any time?" Brooke said.

"Yes. It's easiest when you know who you want to watch—"

"Like me and Jim?" Brooke interrupted.

Nick nodded and gave her a cheeky grin. "Yeah, like that. But when you don't know who you want to hone in on, you can use a keyword system, kind of like you would on Google."

"I don't understand."

"I still don't either," Nick said. "The first time Jack showed this to me, he had it find me by typing in my name. The picture came up behind me, of me. I obviously thought it was just a camera in the room that he had tapped into. No big technology revelations there. But when he handed me a mobile screen to watch the ASE on, and I took it all around the village and it never lost sight of me, I was a believer.

That, and I typed in the president's name when everyone went to bed. Dude has some weird nighttime habits."

"You watched the president?"

"Yeah, and Jennifer Lopez. But I swear to god I turned it off when she got in the shower."

Brooke raised her eyebrow. "This is . . . How does it work?"

Zeke chimed in. "It works a lot like a radio. Only it works off of *every* type of wave that runs through Earth's atmosphere. It seamlessly converts all of those waves into realtime video and audio. Thus why we can watch this agent walk into an ambush."

Answering Brooke's questions had made Nick forget why they were standing there. It was still hard to compute that it wasn't a movie, or past video surveillance that they were watching.

"We can talk more about this later, Brooke." Nick gave Zeke a pat on the shoulder. "Show me why it's an ambush."

Zeke put his hand on a ball that was sitting in a pod. It reminded Nick of the ball in socket controller used on the arcade game, Golden Tee. He moved it forward and the view moved on the screen, away from the agent, and toward the house he was approaching.

"When I keyed in on the agent's conversation, his handler was telling him that it was confirmed that the target was alone in the house."

Zeke moved the ball some more, until the feed was inside the house. There were armed men at every entrance. A cold chill ran down Nick's spine. He'd been in many ambush situations in his time with the Army and had lost a lot of men to such faulty intel.

Zeke continued. "So I moved forward like this and when

I saw the armed men, I came running to get you. If he goes in there, he's a dead man."

Zeke's words hung in the air as they watched him move the feed back outside to the agent. All three of them watched as he checked the magazine in his pistol, then fitted the end of the gun with a suppressor.

"I've gotta get down there. He's going to get himself killed!" Nick moved over to a table on his right and began filling his utility belt with weapons. First, he holstered a Beretta M9—Army standard issue—the pistol he'd been using for more than two decades, then added two spare magazines, a Chris Reeve Yarborough knife, and of course the double-powered hand grenade that Zeke built. Because, why not? Finally, he pressed a button in the middle of the buckle, and the color of the belt changed from bright white to the green and black camouflage on his pants.

"What are you doing? You can't go down there alone," Brooke said.

"What choice do I have? CIA has a man getting ready to walk into an ambush. I can't leave him hanging."

"Nick, you'll be killed. There were seven men inside there waiting."

"Brooke, this is what I do."

Brooke stepped in front of Nick as he went for the door. "But it's not necessary, Nick. Let me call Agent Andrews and tell him to get word to this agent. We can stop him without you putting yourself in danger."

"Brooke, I'll be there before you even get Andrews on the phone. You're not in the reality that governed how you have always handled threats anymore. That's why I'm choosing to use this . . . *thing* that the old jolly guy passed along to me. Please, just help Zeke find out *why* someone is sending this agent into an ambush. Let me worry about stopping it."

Nick stepped around Brooke and shouted back to Zeke as he walked out. "I'll have you in my ear, Zeke. And I have the mobile ASE on my phone in case we still have to go in."

"But you need clearance to get involved in a CIA mission!"

Nick didn't wait to hear what more Brooke had to say about protocol. It was time to get back to Nick Campos—Army Ranger. The man that would never wait around when there was an ally in danger. And he wasn't about to wait around now.

6

"My agent is right outside the house. Make sure your men kill him. I believe he accessed the information about tomorrow night."

Nasir Samara sat quietly in his bedroom, his heart pounding in anger. It had taken him years to find a way in with someone high enough in the CIA to get information he needed. Now, as he sat there seething, stroking his salt and pepper beard, a sweat building beneath his clothing, he couldn't help but worry it was all for nothing.

Nasir was only about a mile from where Justin Kimber, the American agent, was being led. He'd played this game of cat and mouse with the US government for more than a decade. So far he had been able to out maneuver the "world's greatest military minds". He'd been doing it since the day a few years ago US special operatives invaded his village. Nasir's men had killed more than half of the twelve-man team. All these years later, here he was again, outwitting, and outplaying the War Machine's "intelligence community". But it wouldn't matter if he outplayed the CIA tonight, if it meant tomorrow's festivities would still be ruined.

He also didn't have time to worry about this one measly agent and what he knew. Even if it did stop the attack he'd been planning for Christmas Eve. The information that the CIA agent he had in his pocket had been feeding him over the last couple of months was the real prize. Nasir still wasn't sure if he believed the outlandish tale entirely. In fact, when the agent first brought it to Nasir, he almost killed him on the spot. If it wasn't for what had been happening in the US to some of their FBI's most wanted over the last couple of weeks, he might have ended up disregarding it anyway, despite the hours he'd spent researching a way to steal the supposed technology. But now that he'd seen proof of this—almost alien—cloaking device this so-call Santa Claus character had, he would do anything to get his hands on it. Including all of the smoke and mirrors with this Agent Kimber, to lure *Santa* and his cloaking technology.

"Reckoning?" the agent said in his annoying nasally voice. Reckoning was the name Nasir had chosen to use for himself during communications with the American. Just in case someone else happened to be listening.

"I don't care about this agent," Nasir finally spoke. "I only care if this man from the North Pole your agency has been dealing with takes the bait for the trap we've set. Is he coming?"

"I—I don't know."

"What do you mean you don't know?" Nasir said.

"I mean, I said the words they are supposed to be looking out for, but that doesn't mean they are. Nick said the guy he was working with at the North Pole was sort of a nutcase. He said it was in a good way, but that may mean he didn't follow orders to check for the keywords."

"I don't understand any of this," Nasir said. "I just want this cloaking device."

"The cloaking device is something spectacular, Reckoning. But I'm telling you, this device he's using to literally see *everything*? That's the technology you really want."

Nasir scooted to the edge of the bed and burrowed his feet into his slippers. He wasn't going to get much sleep tonight, so he thought it best to work off some of his nervous energy by pacing the floor.

"If I've learned anything, it's to take things one matter at a time," Nasir said. "Let's concentrate on the cloaking device. Then we can worry about this *witchcraft* you are speaking of."

"Okay. Well, there's no sign of Nick in London yet. But we may not see him at all. The cloak is that good," the agent said.

Nasir walked in a circle around his bedroom. "You said he mentioned something about the cloaking device manipulating radio waves?"

"Yeah. Said it works the same as this all-seeing device. Only instead of using radio frequencies and other things in the atmosphere to see things, the cloaking device simply reverses it so you can't see him."

Nasir was floored that such a thing could actually exist.

"Listen," the agent said. "I know because he is calling himself Santa Claus that he seems like he's going to be some weird and kooky guy. And maybe he is. But he's also an Army Ranger. So you'd better hope if he does show up that your men are good. Because he sure as hell is. Cloaking device or not."

Nasir didn't really know what to think of someone who

said they were actually Santa Claus. But he had faith in his men. Even though the seven he had waiting for agent Kimber in the house just down the road weren't his best men, there were still seven of them, and they had the element of surprise.

"Just get this *Nick* to come to your agent's aid. My men will take care of the rest."

"I'll do my best."

Nasir ended the call with Agent Andrews. He was confident that Andrews would keep their arrangement quiet. Not just because of the money he was paying him for his cooperation, but because Nasir had made it very clear that if he did ever reveal anything, Nasir would disappear and make sure it looked like Andrews was the only one plotting against the Americans.

Nasir walked over to the nightstand, picked up the handheld radio, and pressed the talk button. "The agent is just outside your house. Keep him alive until the man with the cloaking device arrives. When you capture him, call me back. No communication until then."

"Copy. We will have what you want soon."

Nasir set down the radio. Now that he had done all he could do for the night's little confrontation, it was time to focus on tomorrow. He was ready to deliver a Christmas present the United States of America would never forget.

7

NICK HAD HIS HANDS ON THE REINS, BUT IT WASN'T necessary. Like a GPS, the reindeer already knew the coordinates. The sleigh was on autopilot and had just dipped below the clouds enough to see the lights of London shimmering through the rain. Every time Nick came out of a cloud like this, it reminded him of when he first saw the sleigh falling from the sky a year ago. After learning about the space-age cloaking device, he didn't understand why he'd been able to see Santa fall that night in the desert. When he asked Jack about it, he didn't have a good answer for it. Mrs. Claus, of course, in all her positivity, told Nick she believed Santa had done it on purpose. Saying that she thought Santa had *chosen* Nick. Nick thought that sounded nice, and it probably made Mrs. Claus feel better, but if Santa's objective was to *choose* someone to carry on delivering presents and being jolly, there wasn't a chance in hell he would have chosen Nick.

Whatever the case might have been, there was Nick, flying through the air on the "present plane", two days before Christmas, with a sack full of the best weapons money could buy and a mind full of violence. The lights of the city below were behind him now, and the reindeer pointed their antlers toward the ground. Nick checked his belt. All of his weaponry was there. Out of habit, he pulled his Beretta, and ensured that a round was waiting in the chamber. It was, and the suppressor was twisted tight at the end of the barrel.

"Okay, Nick, looks like you're getting there just in time," Zeke's voice came through Nick's earpiece. "Agent Kimber has just climbed over the back wall. He's ducked behind two garbage bins and is staring at the back door. He might be ready to make a move. You'd better get in there."

"What's going on inside?" Nick said.

"A man at the front and back door. Two at the windows on the left side of the house, and two on the right. One guy in the—oh god! That's disgusting!"

"What? What is it? Is someone hurt?" Nick felt for his phone in his pocket so he could take a look at the ASE himself.

"Ewe, no! The seventh guy is in the bathroom and I saw the massive—"

"Zeke!"

"Thank god there's no smell on the ASE. Oh god that is—"

"Zeke! This isn't playtime. People's lives are on the line. Put Brooke on the mic and help her navigate the ASE. You aren't ready for this."

"But—."

"Put Brooke on now, or I'm putting you back in the toy assembly line."

Nick knew this wasn't going to be like working with the Rangers, but he hadn't realized just how unequipped he'd left Zeke to handle this. Training on the COMS was never something Nick had done in the Army. He was always in the field. Thank god he had Brooke there. She'd been a cop before she moved to the FBI.

"This is Brooke. How can I help?"

"You've done some tactical training, right?"

"You mean you don't already know that, Santa?"

"Really, Brooke? You're going to do this right now?"

"No, just trying to relax you." Her tone switched into FBI mode. "The seventh man in the house is walking upstairs. I think that's where you should start. Zeke, show me the outside of the house. Nick, I'll find you a way up."

"No need," Zeke's voice came through. "He can just land on the roof."

For a moment, Nick's mind was blown. This entire Santa Claus setup was perfect for taking down criminals. The slightest trickle of something he couldn't put his finger on seeped into his consciousness. The words of Mrs. Claus saying Nick had been chosen replayed in his head.

"Nick, you have to get down there. Agent Kimber is about to move."

Nick shook the odd feeling and stood on the sled to see over the reindeer. "The roof," he told them. Then the sled dipped even farther, like they were going to crash headfirst into the ground. They were still moving at breakneck speed, and the ground was closing in. Nick's stomach began to turn as his grip became so tight around the reins that if felt as if his flesh would rip. Just as he was about to shout something, anything, at them, the reindeer leveled out and practically floated onto the roof of the house.

Nick took a deep breath to calm his nerves. "Really, guys?" he said to the reindeer. He only got a few snorts back in return.

"Nick," Brooke said. "The agent has moved to the side of

the house. If you don't hurry, he's going to walk right into a hailstorm of bullets."

Nick stepped down from the sleigh and focused Brooke. "Where is the man upstairs?"

"Top floor. It's a bedroom. How are you going to get in the house?"

Nick walked over to the edge of the roof and looked down. There was a window just below him. Then he looked back to the roof, over to his right. Brooke must have been looking at the same thing with the ASE. "Nick, you're not actually going to use the chimney, are you?"

The thought had crossed his mind on the ride there. Or at least the thought of how it might actually work. "I feel like it's a right of passage," he said.

"Nick," Brooke chided.

"Come on, Brooke. Didn't Jim ever let you have any fun when you were running down bad guys?"

"Nick!"

"All right. No. I'm not taking the chimney." He looked back over the edge of the roof. There was a ledge protruding from the window. "And noted. You never had any fun while doing your job."

8

NICK BENT DOWN, GOT A SOLID GRIP ON THE GUTTER THAT ran along the underside of the roof above the window, and lowered himself down. The rain had picked up a bit since landing on the roof. The drops were cold against the back of his neck. Despite the wet conditions, he was able to get good footing on the ledge with the balls of his feet. With his left hand gripping the shutter, he tested the window—locked. But he'd been planning to break the window from the moment he saw it, so this didn't deter him. He wanted the attention of the seven cowards awaiting the American agent to be on him upstairs instead.

As if Brooke knew exactly what he needed, she chimed in through the earpiece. "One of the terrorists has just sat down on the bed in the room. He'll be a little to your right when you make it through the window. Now would be a good time to go."

Their working relationship might actually have a chance to succeed.

Nick readied his pistol. He was going to kick in the

window, front-roll with his arms out in front of him, then crouch on a knee to take his shot. He pulled his boot back—

"Wait, Nick!" Brooke said.

Nick was mid kick, but was just able to stop his boot from making contact with the glass. He was breathing heavily from his heightened adrenaline, but he held position and waited for Brooke's instruction.

"He's off the bed and walking toward the window. Nick, he's headed right for you!"

Nick put his foot back on the ledge. He let Brooke's voice fade and his instinct take over. He crouched down and moved the tip of his pistol to the center of the window.

"Nick!"

The curtains on the other side of the window that kept Nick from seeing inside began to move. Nick squeezed the trigger twice, rose up, and smashed his boot through the window. The crash was loud in the quiet house, and tiny shards of broken glass tap danced across the hardwood floor below him. The glow from the streetlamp behind him shined through the window, illuminating the man writhing on the floor holding both hands to his neck.

Nick stepped inside and bent down beside him. For a moment Nick forgot the man couldn't see him as the man looked to the broken window for who had shot him. The cloaking device was deceiving to Nick's eye. He could still see himself, so it was easy to forget that no one else could. Jack had mentioned this was the way Santa was able to place presents under the tree without ever being noticed. Nick once again was baffled that the fat man hadn't shared any of this technology with the US military. Regardless, he was certainly happy to be wearing the invisibility now. He could move down the stairs as if he were a ghost.

The footsteps coming up the stairs refocused Nick, and

so did Brooke's update. "Two men coming your way. Agent Kimber has just picked the lock. He's going in. They'll kill him if he doesn't get help!"

Nick left the dying man to wonder about the ghost of Christmas present that had just put a hole in his throat and moved to the open bedroom door. He could hear the two men plodding up the stairs.

"Jalal!" one of the men screamed. Then he shouted something else Nick didn't understand. But it didn't matter what he said, because they were the last words he ever spoke.

Nick dropped to a knee and shot both men dead as they ran into the room. It was like shooting balloons at a carnival. Nick almost felt bad about the invisible advantage he had. *Almost*. The gunfire that erupted downstairs stripped those feelings completely.

He stepped over the men. Each had taken two in the chest. As he rushed down the stairs, he swapped for a fresh magazine. His first one wasn't empty, but a long time ago, when Nick and his tactical team were clearing a house in Iraq, he'd made the mistake of trying to finish a magazine before reloading. When the slide locked back on his pistol after only four spent rounds, he took a bullet in the shoulder for his mistake. When the medic was shoving tweezers down into his soft tissue an hour later to retrieve the embedded bullet as he bit down on a leather belt, he vowed to not be so careless again.

Brooke said, "There's a man on your right at the bottom of the stairs. He's getting ready to walk into the hallway and surprise the agent!"

With a fresh magazine locked and a round in the chamber, Nick came around the corner of the stairs, and shot the man on his right twice in the arm and shoulder. He scanned to his right, but when he turned back to the hallway agent Kimber was wearing a look of shock on his face as he kept his gun trained on the bottom of the stairs, right where Nick stood. Nick might have been invisible to the human eye, but a bullet would still tear right through him.

"That's everyone. Nick, you did it!" Brooke said.

Nick heard her, but he was focused on Agent Kimber. Kimber's finger was caressing the trigger. Nick backed up to the landing halfway up the stairs and moved around the corner of the wall. Just in case.

"Army Ranger Nick Campos," Nick shouted. "Put your weapon down."

"Bullshit," Kimber shouted. His voice was shaky. "CIA, come out with your hands up."

Nick peeked around the corner. Kimber's weapon was still fixed on the stairs. He was a fairly young man—maybe thirty—dark hair and wide eyes. He was dressed in all black tactical gear.

"The house is clear, son," Nick said. "I've got three down upstairs. You were sent into an ambush."

"Impossible."

"What the hell do you think happened then? You think these armed men were here to help you get the job done?" There was a groan from the man Nick shot in the arm. "He was going to kill you, you know. I made sure he didn't."

Agent Kimber moved over to the man down and picked up his weapon. "Just stay right there. Do not move, or I will shoot you."

Nick moved onto the landing to get a better view. Now that Kimber had moved out of the hallway, Nick was clear at the top of the landing. Kimber was holding the gun to the injured man's head.

"Don't shoot him," Nick said. "I need to know who set you up. Maybe he'll talk."

Nick eased his way downstairs. The steps creaked under his feet, and Agent Kimber reacted by swinging the gun toward the stairs.

"I said don't move!"

It was hard for Nick to keep moving with the gun pointed straight at him. But he had to trust that when the agent saw nothing, he wouldn't shoot.

"And it's not your business what I do." Kimber pointed the gun back at the injured man, who let out another grunt of pain. "I'm CIA. Whatever reason you're here, you don't have clearance."

Nick now stood right in front of the agent. He reached up, bent his wrist back, and twisted the slide of the pistol as he pulled it free. The agent leapt back in fear.

"You're right, I don't have clearance. I have carte blanche." Nick pressed the button on the fob in his pocket, and the agent's face went white when Nick appeared with his gun pointed right at him. "Freaky, right?"

The agent reached for his pocket where he had stashed the injured man's gun.

"Don't," Nick said. "I'm not here to kill you. If I was, you'd already be dead."

9

NICK WASN'T SURE ABOUT A LOT OF THINGS IN LIFE, BUT AS HE
steered the reindeer back down to the North Pole, he was a
hundred percent certain that until now, there had never
been a half-dead terrorist riding in the back of ol' Santa's
sleigh. Mrs. Claus was not going to be happy about this.
And neither was Jack. Jack was already upset that Brooke
was there. He said the entire point of operating from the
North Pole was to keep the mystique, and the more people
that had actually seen it, the more the romance of the story
died. Though Nick thought Jack—the king of the elves—
was being dramatic, he also supposed it was true. The two
new fresh faces coming down with the sleigh were going to
really set him off. Nick had always had a knack for causing
trouble. Why would things change now?

"What the actual f—" Agent Kimber would have
finished his sentence, but just like everyone else, the sight of
Santa's village took his breath away.

The novelty had already worn off for Nick. He wasn't
going to explain the *magic* of the North Pole to anyone else.

Agent Kimber would have to fill in the blanks himself sometime later. There was too much to do. The sleigh pulled in over by Warehouse Z this time. Nick didn't have time to explain things to Jack and Mrs. Claus either. It was clear from Nick's brief conversation with Agent Kimber— after he finally calmed down from seeing the invisible man earlier—that the US intelligence community had some serious holes in it. More importantly, Nick was still reeling from the revelation that Nasir Samara had been Kimber's target back at the house outside London.

Nick was all too familiar with that name. Nasir had come across his path on more than one occasion while he'd hunted terrorists as a Ranger. The last time it had, Nick's closest friend ended up dead. Nick was seething as he hopped off the sleigh. He grabbed the injured man from the back and ripped him from his seat down to the snowy ground below. Agent Kimber was trying to talk to Nick, but Nick wasn't paying any attention. Instead, he hoisted the terrorist up—practically carrying him to the warehouse— shoved open the door, and threw him inside.

Brooke and Zeke jumped up from the ASE station and rushed over.

"Everybody out!" Nick shouted. His voice echoed through the warehouse.

"Nick—" Brooke started, but the look Nick shot her cut her off.

The playfully bantering fun-time-guy Nick had been with Brooke up to that point was gone. And she caught her first glimpse of the man Nick had grown to be over the last twenty years of service. Brooke patted Zeke on the shoulder. Zeke made a happy *ALL RIGHT!* face at Nick and gave him two thumbs up as he moved with Brooke toward the exit.

Nick looked over at Agent Kimber, who was taking in all of the gadgets in the large open room.

"You've been studying these guys," Nick said. "Snap out of your fairytale trance and get this asshole to talk. If I do it, I'll kill him. Interrogations aren't my forté."

Kimber was still fixated on the Iron Santa suit a few feet away.

"Agent Kimber!"

Nick's shout finally snapped him out of it, and Kimber's CIA mind finally kicked back in.

"Right, sorry. My brain is still playing catch up." Kimber circled around the man on the floor, putting his back to the things in the warehouse that were distracting him. "I've been watching Nasir's movements for over a year now myself. Well, trying to. He's rather elusive."

Not for long, Nick thought as he glanced over at the ASE.

Kimber continued. "Intelligence has shown a lot of movement into the outskirts of London. Some of his known associates had been spotted near where we were earlier. A fellow agent captured part of a conversation saying that something was planned . . ." Kimber pulled his phone from his pocket and checked the clock. ". . . for today. Now. Christmas Eve. Then my handler made contact just a bit ago saying they had Nasir alone in the house we just came from."

"Kill order?" Nick said.

Kimber nodded.

"Your handler's a double agent."

Kimber's head swiveled to meet Nick's eyes. "No chance."

"How else do you explain the 'intel' being so far off base? You were setup, Bub."

Kimber circled back around the man on the floor, who

was going in and out of consciousness. "Not Andrews. He's a weasel, but he's not a traitor."

Now it was Nick who was shocked. "Andrews? Donald Andrews? *He's* your handler?"

"What, you know him?"

"Know him? He's my liaison with CIA Director Simpson."

Both men were quiet for a moment. Nick's mind was racing. It was juggling his anger at the man responsible for his friend's death and Andrews betrayal of his country. His betrayal of Nick. Nick wasn't sure who he was going to swoop down and kill first, but he was positive that both his enemies would get theirs before the night was through.

"I don't understand," Kimber said. "Why would Andrews do this?"

"Why does anyone turn? It happens every day."

"Not in the CIA it doesn't."

Nick raised an eyebrow when Kimber looked his way. Then when Nick looked down at the terrorist, a bolt of anger flashed through him, and so did the face of his fallen friend. Nick pulled his strap, took a knee beside the man on the ground, and squeezed his throat with his left hand while he put his Beretta to the man's temple with his right.

"What is your coward boss planning?" Nick shouted. The man's eyes opened. There was no fear to be found; only contempt. When he didn't answer, Nick squeezed harder. "Answer me!"

"Nick!" Kimber shouted.

The terrorist's face had turned a bright shade of maroon. Nick only squeezed harder. The man's eyes began to bulge.

"Nick! If you kill him, we'll never find Nasir!"

Nick released his grip and stood. "I don't need him to

tell me where Nasir is. How do you think I found you?" By the quizzical look on Kimber's face, Nick could tell the thought had never occurred to him. "All that matters to me is stopping whatever they've planned. Dealing with Andrews and Nasir will be the easy part."

10

"What do you mean he's not dead?"

If Agent Andrew's voice had been squeaky before, the fear took it almost to a shriek. Nasir was worried about the implications of Agent Kimber's survival too, but he wasn't going to let the agent know it. The agent didn't know half of what Nasir was up to. All Nasir wanted to do was find out where the man with the cloaking device—the one who dismantled Nasir's seven-man team—was going to be next. It was clear that this thing that could make him invisible was well worth any amount of work it would be to find him and take it from him. No matter how dangerous that might be.

"Looks like your days with the CIA are numbered. Which means you are no longer of use to me." Nasir ended the call. He didn't want to hear the agent begging him for his life. He had much bigger things to focus on. Besides, he had already dispatched someone to take care of Andrews.

Nasir wasn't going to get any sleep, that much he could tell. Not until he got on the jet registered to his shell company, and flew over to Washington D.C. The five-hour time difference from London would give him plenty of time to make it there for the evening's festivities. The difference now was that the cloaking device would guarantee that he could do the damage he'd hoped to do.

He walked over to the armoire and switched the radio jammer back on. He'd been using them for years, but after Agent Andrews talked of this All-Seeing device, and said that it used radio waves to see, his love for jammers would have to now become an obsession. Nasir had no choice but to begin taking every precaution. Fortunately, he was prepared to become "invisible" himself. Over the years, a man such as himself had always been a heavy target to the United States. Their technology had been finding him more than he cared to think about. That was the reason he'd taken measures to fight against those weapons and listening devices. And it was the reason he'd had the jammers and carried them with him everywhere he went. They had never been more useful than they would be now.

It was clear to Nasir that the American agent that was at the house about a mile from him had had help. Nasir's two other men that were watching the house hadn't seen another operative, yet the second floor window crashed inward all on its own, and the agent and one of Nasir's men had disappeared without a trace. His men were frightened, but Nasir knew it was the man with the cloaking device. The man they were calling Saint Nick had found the agent and helped him after all. Andrews' plan had worked to lure Nick there to the house.

Nasir couldn't do anything about the fact that his men were dead, but with this radio wave jammer, he hoped he could at least keep Nick from seeing where he was. Nasir still didn't understand how it was possible to use radio waves to see and hear from so far away, but now that

Andrews' intel had shown it to be true, and after this Nick came in as the invisible man, he had no choice but to believe Andrews about the all-seeing eye technology. The cloaking device was unbelievable. But Andrews had been right—this all-seeing device was the real prize, and Nasir *had* to have it.

CIA Agent Kimber, the man that Nick saved, might tell Nick and the rest of the CIA all about Nasir's plans for an attack on the White House set for later that evening now that things had gone awry. Which was exactly why Nasir let Agent Kimber come across that information. Nasir had learned that anything said over open airwaves was dangerous. But if you knew the CIA was listening, you could use that to your benefit. Now that Nasir knew Nick would be going to stop Nasir's plan of attack at the White House, he could set a trap for Nick and take the technology from him. And still be able to make sure the real damage to the Americans was done. He had never gone to personally carry out any of his attacks, but this one . . . this one was special.

Nasir couldn't help but smile. After a lifetime of desire had burned inside him to strike a blow against the evil Western Culture, he was finally going to get his chance. Not only would the attack be against America's most beloved person, but it would also be the largest attack in history on American soil. He had never liked Christmas—in fact he loathed the materialistic sins of the holiday—but after tonight, and after getting his hands on technology that would inflict even greater harm in the years to come, Nasir thought he just might become a fan of the ridiculous Christian holiday.

11

"What do you mean you can't find him?" Nick was incensed. "This thing's called the All-Seeing Eye, right? ALL SEEING?"

"Boss," Zeke said. "I'm trying what always works, but I can't find him. Did you drop your cloaking device or something?"

"No," Nick said, but it was almost a subconscious answer. When you've been around the highest levels of the military for as long as Nick had been, you learn a lot about technology. At least about the tech used for the purposes of war. He knew that a lot of the communication devices and even vehicles the Army used overseas were wrapped in a material made to block radio waves in case of an EMP attack, which would render anything electronic useless. The materials covering them would help keep them running after an EMP blast if there ever was one. He also heard of suits made of the same material to keep radiation from harming soldiers. And that it also helped keep them from being heard over communications. Or, it could be something ridiculously analogue like a frequency jammer.

Zeke and Nick hadn't tested whether they stopped the ASE from seeing, but Nick had a hunch something like that would if it interrupted radio signals.

Zeke grunted. "Maybe he has elves too."

Nick didn't pay the idiotic comment any attention.

"If Andrews is his informant . . ." Brooke spoke up, ". . . Isn't it likely that he told Nasir about your All-Seeing Eye?"

"Go on," Nick said. Brooke was even sharper than he thought.

"Well, if Andrews told him how it works, he would know how to block it. It's not new technology to have radio-wave-blocking material or jamming devices. Criminals use it all the time when they don't want us at the FBI listening in. A guy like Nasir would surely have such things to keep his communications safe."

"I knew I brought you along for a reason," Nick said. He was impressed.

"You mean other than your childish game of 'gotcha back' you were playing with Jim?"

Nick was ready with another smartass remark, but there was a knock at the warehouse door. Nick walked over to the door. "Zeke, I think Brooke is right. Nasir has found a way to keep us from seeing him. Find another way in."

Nick opened the door to find Jack and Mrs. Claus standing there in the snow with their arms folded across their chests.

"You can't come in here right now."

Mrs. Claus gasped. Nick noticed she was looking over his shoulder. He had forgotten that the bloody terrorist was tied to a chair in eyeshot of the doorway. Mrs. Claus pushed her way through the doorway.

Agent Kimber's mouth hung open as a subconscious

thought slipped from his mouth. "You have got to be kidding me."

Mrs. Claus's voice went up an octave. "Nick, what are you doing here? You can't turn this village into a war zone!" She walked right over to the man and assessed him. Her normally rosy and chubby cheeks now looked like they were on fire against her pale skin. Her long white hair was in a bun, and she clutched the lapels of her reindeer-embroidered white robe against her chest. "Oh, you poor man. We must get him to Doctor Rubins immediately."

"Don't you feel sorry for him, Mary. He's the scum of the earth."

She whirled around wearing a scowl. "Nick! How dare you speak like that?"

"He's a terrorist, Mary. This isn't one of your husband's naughty list moments. The guy doesn't pick on Sally in the schoolyard. He kills innocent people. Lots of them."

Her lips went from fiercely pursed to fully pouting. She looked at the man, then back to Nick. "I will NOT have this here at the village. You will *not* tarnish my husband's legacy. I took you in like a son when you came here a year ago with the most horrible news I will ever receive. Ever since then, you haven't so much as mentioned what you are to do tonight! What you are *supposed* to do tonight. And now . . . This?"

Nick was truly at a loss. "What I'm supposed to do tonight? I don't understand. What do you mean?"

Now sadness was the only emotion left on Mrs. Claus' face. "It's Christmas Eve, Nick. You're supposed to be delivering cheer to boys and girls all across the world. Instead . . . you bring this . . . violence?"

Now Nick was upset. "There are people that are going to die tonight because of this man and who he works for, and you want to talk to me about presents and Christmas carols? You live on another planet, Mary. You have no idea how the real world works, and neither did your husband." Nick began to pace. "Presents? Really?"

Brooke walked over and put her arm around Mrs. Claus. As she did this, she gave Nick a look that could kill. Nick realized he was talking to someone who really didn't have a clue, who was the sweetest lady on Earth, and that he had made a mistake. But he didn't have time for this. People's lives were really at stake.

"It's all right . . . Mary is it?" Brooke told her. Mrs. Claus nodded. "You have to understand the world that Nick is coming from. It's not like it is here. You can't expect him to understand why tonight is so important to you if you can't understand why keeping people safe is important to him. It's all he's ever known."

Mrs. Claus' face softened. She looked up at Nick, and he stopped pacing. "You don't think I know? You don't think I've seen why my husband wanted so desperately to have one night of cheer? He knew what evil was going on out there. That's why what he did was so important. So people could escape all the terrible things. At least for one night."

Nick walked over to her. "But Mary, I can't turn a blind eye to those things. If I do, those presents that your husband wanted so desperately to give to the children to cheer them up? They won't be able to get them, because they'll be dead."

Mrs. Claus began to cry.

"Can't you see you're upsetting her?" Little Jack walked up and stepped between them. "Back off, Nick!"

Before Nick could react, Mrs. Claus placed her hand on Jack's shoulder. "It's all right, Jack. As much as I wish it weren't true, Nick is right. I just never thought it would come to our doorstep here in the village. I wanted to shelter everyone from such things. I see now that maybe that was wrong of me ... wrong of my husband."

She wept.

"No, Mary," Brooke said. "It takes all kinds of people to make the world go 'round. What you and your husband have created here is just as important as what Nick does. Probably more so. You give people hope."

"Yeah, well, Nick doesn't think so. And he is the one my husband chose to pass this along too. Why, I don't know. But he did."

Brooke took Mary's hands in her own. "Maybe this is why, Mary. Maybe your husband knew all along he could have been doing more. Maybe in the end he decided to do something about it?"

Everyone in the warehouse was speechless. For a moment Nick thought maybe she was right. Mary walked over and gave Nick a hug. "It's all right, Nick. Do what you have to do. I guess there is always next year for the children to get their gifts."

Nick felt something funny move over him. He wasn't sure what it was ... but he suddenly wondered if he actually cared what this lady was feeling. Somewhere inside him, he probably did, but it wouldn't come to the surface on this night. Nick had to get a plan together for D.C. If the president was possibly in danger, he couldn't let *feelings* get in the way of saving him. He had to get to Andrews to learn more about what Nasir was planning. Mrs. Claus could go back to baking gingerbread cookies in her cozy little world. Nick had to go to war in his.

He pulled himself away from Mrs. Claus. "I'm sorry I don't understand why not delivering presents is a big deal. There are peoples' lives at stake."

Nick walked toward the ASE and he caught a glimpse of Brooke on the way there. She clearly was not happy with him. *Join the club,* Nick thought.

"Now if everyone can please leave us. We have real problems to deal with here."

Mrs. Claus hung her head and walked with Jack over to the door. "Just be careful, Nick. My husband thought there was something special about you. I hope he was right."

Nick was already in go-mode. "Zeke, pull up Agent Andrews. He's our first stop on the reckoning tour."

The door to the warehouse shut.

Brooke walked over to the ASE. "You didn't have to treat her like that. She doesn't understand—"

Nick turned and interrupted. "Yeah, well maybe it's time she woke up."

"Why? So she can be like you, Nick? Mad at the world? Treating everyone else like they are the enemy if they don't think like you do?"

"I don't really care, Brooke." Nick turned back to the ASE. "Go bake cookies with her if you feel bad. You of all people should understand. You are around criminals every day."

"You're right, Nick. I am. But that doesn't mean I let them jade my outlook. That doesn't mean I don't believe in things that are good."

Nick turned back to her, a confident, arrogant look on his face. "I'm the good in the world this Christmas. Someone who is going to stop people from dying. Not some fat son of a bitch who gives presents to kids that will one day try to blow us all up. I live in reality. And if you don't mind, I've got work to do."

12

NICK, BROOKE, AGENT KIMBER, AND ZEKE SPENT THE NEXT few hours combing through data with the ASE. Nick had Jack take the terrorist they'd brought back from London down to the States and drop him outside of CIA headquarters. When they searched for Agent Andrews with the ASE to see what he was up to, there was no sign of him. Nick knew what that meant, but Brooke had someone from LAPD go by Andrews' house to make sure. The report back was that the front door had been kicked in and he had been shot three times. Dead. You do business with a terrorist, that is eventually how you will end up.

As far as Nasir Samara was concerned, they still couldn't find him either. But according to Agent Kimber, he was more than likely on his way to the US. More specifically, to Washington D.C. There was something Nick didn't like about what Agent Kimber had found out. Something smelt a little fishy. Nick had been studying and fighting terrorists for two decades, and in all that time, he had never seen the leader of any terror organization take the chance of coming to US soil. They always sat in their bunkers like some villain in a comic book and made their cronies go out and do the dirty work. Kimber saying that he actually heard a recording of Nasir talking about personally coming to D.C. set off all kinds of alarm bells in Nick's brain.

Someone like Nasir, who had been keeping secrets from secret agents all his life, didn't let people record his conversations. And even if there actually was a recording, Nasir would never be dumb enough to openly talk about plans. He would never mention actual locations. He would use codewords. And he would never, *ever* talk about where he was going to be. Whether it was a rathole in the mountains or a major city in the United States, those words would never leave his lips on a telephone call. Never.

So what did that mean to Nick? He still wasn't sure. That was why the last couple of hours they'd been combing through the ASE for known associates of Nasir, or of Agent Andrews. Trying desperately to find *anyone* who might be talking about what is really happening. So far, they'd found nothing.

Nick walked over to Agent Kimber and kicked the leg of the folding chair he was sleeping in. Kimber almost fell out of the chair as he woke up with a start.

"Tell me again about how you came across this conversation Nasir had about D.C."

"Nick," Brooke walked over. "Is this really necessary? Shouldn't we be contacting people in D.C. to get prepared for an attack?"

Nick didn't even look her way. His eyes stayed focused on Kimber, who rubbed his face with both hands as he tried to wake himself up. "How'd you hear this conversation?"

Out of the corner of his eye, he saw Brooke throw up her hands and walk away in a huff to make some more coffee.

Kimber stood up. "I told you, Agent Andrews had an

agent combing the phone taps in London. He came across a call where D.C. was mentioned and he recorded the call. It was sent to me, and I heard Nasir telling his pilot to get the plane ready for Washington. That's why Agent Andrews had me move on Nasir."

"Yeah, only you didn't move on Nasir. You moved on seven of his men who were waiting there to kill you."

The room was quiet.

Nick stared a hole through Kimber as he waited patiently for him to say something else.

"What?" Kimber held out his arms. "You know the rest. You bailed me out."

"Really? That's all you've got?" Nick said.

"What do you mean?"

"You're lying."

"Nick?" Brooke spoke up.

Nick took a step closer to Kimber. "Either you're lying, or Agent Andrews was lying. Or both. Which is it?"

"I'm not going to stand here and be accused of treason by Santa Claus and his dwarfs." Kimber backed away and reached in his pocket. "I'm going for a smoke."

Nick reached out to grab him, but Brooke caught his arm and stepped in between. "What are you doing, Nick? Just because we can't find answers doesn't mean you can force them."

Brooke's eyes were bloodshot. It had been a long night, so Nick decided he would give her a pass on stepping in for that reason only. "Don't step in when I am talking to someone again, Brooke. Understand?"

Brooke took a step back. "Excuse me? You're not my boss. And you won't talk to me like that. I'm just trying to get you to use some reason here."

"What the hell do you know about any of this? What

makes you think you can tell me how to handle it? I've been dealing with guys like Nasir for years. They are smarter than you think. We know he got to Andrews, what makes you think he couldn't get to Kimber too?"

Brooke was quiet for a moment.

"Boss," Zeke said from behind them. "You need to see this."

"Not now, Zeke. The adults are having a conversation."

Nick watched Brooke's eyes focus over his shoulder. "Who are you following, Zeke?" Brooke said.

Nick whirled around and the screen showed Kimber walking away from the warehouse. Then he raised a phone to his ear. Nick rushed forward. "Make sure we can hear."

Zeke zoomed in and twisted a knob on the controls. Kimber's voice was loud enough now to hear him.

"No, I'm telling you, he is on to us."

Nick shot a look at Brooke. She hung her head.

Kimber continued his conversation. "You can't just leave me stranded here." Pause. "The North Pole! I have no way out. I came here by sleigh for god's sake! You can't—"

The three of them watched as Kimber took the phone from his ear, looked at it, then put it back to his ear. "Hello! Hello?!" Then he shouted in frustration and put his phone away. He was cursing to himself as he walked down the main street in the village. Nick pulled his Beretta and checked the mag.

"What are you going to do?" Brooke asked.

"What do you think?"

"I don't know, Nick. You're kind of a loose cannon. He doesn't know for sure that we know anything."

"Yes he does. And he's going to get desperate." Nick looked over at Zeke. "Is Jack back yet with the sleigh?"

"I saw him pulling into the stables on camera seven

about a half hour ago. He should be finished putting away the reindeer."

Just as Zeke finished his sentence, Nick watched Kimber walk up to Jack on the ASE's main screen. Then Kimber pulled a gun.

Nick looked at Brooke as he started for the door. "You think I'm the loose cannon?"

"Nick, be careful. He's a highly trained assassin."

"Well what the hell do you think I am?"

Brooke had nothing to say to that. Nick opened the door. "He's going to try to get out of here. Zeke, get Brooke over to the stables. I'd lay money on Kimber trying to make Jack take him to the States. Find a place in there where he can't see you, and make sure he doesn't leave. No matter what you have to do."

"Where are you going?" Brooke asked.

"To try to beat him there."

13

NICK HAD LEFT IN SUCH A RUSH THAT HE'D FORGOTTEN HIS coat. Which would have been fine if it was just cold out, but at the North Pole, cold wasn't thirty degrees, it was thirty below. He was lucky that it was a little warmer tonight, but a still frozen negative three. The snow was lightly falling, and the wind was whipping at his back as he jogged down the alley. His bare arms were already stinging, and he had just left the warm warehouse. It was too late to worry about that now; he had to focus on getting to Kimber.

He came to the edge of the warehouse and stopped. He knew Kimber would have Jack take him to the stables. They were the equivalent of four city blocks from Nick. He saw only an empty side road that was now covered in snow. He followed the only tracks in them—Kimber's footsteps—and crossed to the next alley. At the end of the building was the road where they'd watched Kimber greet Jack with his pistol.

Zeke would be taking Brooke the opposite way around. It was a more direct route to the stables. Nick put it in high gear and ran right across the street where Kimber met Jack, and on through to the other side. When he peered across the next street, he was just able to see the back of Kimber as he pushed Jack into the backside of some of the elves' apartments. Nick ran around the right side of the apartments to try to head Kimber off. He tried not to let the cold bother him, but he was freezing. His teeth began to chatter, and his entire body was shaking.

Nick streaked under a streetlamp and ran up the sidewalk adjacent to the main road. Kimber would have to cross here to get to the stables. Nick ran up to a tree and stood for a moment, waiting for Kimber. He should have already been trying to cross the street. If Jack was his normal stubborn self and put up a fight, Kimber would shoot him. Nick felt his body beginning the process of shutting down from the cold. He had to keep moving.

That was when he heard two gunshots echo through the quiet night. They came from behind the apartments. Nick surged forward, just in time to see the edge of Kimber's coat poke out of the shadows of the apartments. Nick raised his gun and fired twice. Both rounds hit the logs that made up the end of the housing complex—Kimber had recoiled just in time. Nick knew what was coming next. He was completely exposed.

Nick dove for the bush to his left just as he saw Kimber move out of the darkness into the glow of the streetlight. A millisecond later, he heard three shots fire. Nick slid headfirst into the bush. He didn't feel the ripping burn of a bullet, but he did feel sting of the cold and wet snow beneath his already half frozen body.

The cloaking device.

Nick reached in his pocket and felt for the fob. His hand came up empty. An image of his coat lying on one of the chairs in the warehouse flashed in his mind. Not only had forgetting his coat left him freezing cold, it left him without an advantage. A situation Nick had been in many times before.

"Time to go old school," he whispered aloud as he picked himself up from the snow.

"I just want to get out of here, Nick," Kimber shouted from the shadows. "No one else has to get hurt!"

Nick answered by moving his pistol just above the bush he was crouched behind and squeezing the trigger twice. He followed that with a quick glance that only showed him the building. No Kimber. Since he had Brooke waiting at the stables, he could take a chance and try to go around behind Kimber. As he turned and raced back the way he came, he couldn't help but picture Jack dead in the snow. Later he would feel bad for bringing violence to such an innocent place, but right then he had to stay focused so no one else got hurt.

He felt like he was barely moving. The cold made it an act of congress to keep his legs in motion. As he ran down the street at the front of the apartment building, his arms had gone numb. While Nick was used to spending most of his time in miserably hot weather, he had heard on many occasions that bare skin in temperatures below zero didn't take long to get frost bitten. And he'd read one of the first signs was numbness. Not good.

Still, Nick plodded forward through the ankle-high snow. He flailed his arms about as he ran, trying to keep some blood moving through them. He looked right as he passed an alley and caught a glimpse of Kimber. Nick had gotten ahead of him a bit. He dug deep and found another gear. Kimber was running in the direction of Mrs. Claus' house. The last thing he wanted was to bring this to her front door; especially if it put her in danger.

He sped forward, then turned down the first alley on his right. He continued his slow churning sprint down the alley. His lungs were on fire from the cold air he was sucking in, but he couldn't slow down. Nick knew if he was hurting, Kimber had to be about to break. Even if he was more appropriately dressed for the cold, he hadn't been through the wars Nick had been through.

Kimber streaked by, right in front of Nick, and at the last second, Nick dove and managed to grip the back of Kimber's coat collar and drag him to the ground. Normally, Nick would have just shot Kimber, but while he knew what the conversation he overheard Kimber having with the ASE meant, he didn't have proof—yet.

As both men hit the snow, they slid, Nick on his back and Kimber on top of him. As Nick was hooking his right leg around Kimber to secure position, Kimber turned into him. The move surprised Nick. He wasn't expecting Kimber to be versed in Brazilian Jiu-Jitsu. It would be the last time Nick would underestimate him.

Nick wrapped his arms around Kimber, squeezed him close, a defensive move to keep Kimber from posturing up, and to keep him from being able to drop punches down on him. However, his squeeze was weak, as his arms had completely lost feeling. He had almost no power in them at all. Kimber slipped out of his grip, sat up on top of him, and the first punch came downward. Under a normal setting, it would have been easy for Nick to get his arms in front of his face to block, but they were so stiff, he was a split second too late. Kimber's right hand thudded into his forehead. The man hit harder than what he looked capable of. Fist number two from Kimber's oncoming left was on its way down. Nick bucked his hips to throw Kimber off balance, and thankfully the punch went high into the snow above his head.

Kimber recovered quickly, but this time when he raised up, two gunshots broke the silent night, and Kimber dove off of Nick. Nick looked to his left. Down the street, Brooke was glowing under a streetlamp, and she fired two more shots in Kimber's direction. Nick sat up, his body in slow motion, and reached for Kimber as Kimber got to his feet. He was just able to grab an ankle, but Kimber easily pulled away. At that point, Nick's arms were useless, so much so that he wasn't sure if he had even been able to squeeze Kimber's leg at all.

Nick heard two more shots, but Kimber kept running. Brooke made it to Nick just as he picked up the gun that he'd dropped in the tussle and got back up to his feet. She wrapped his coat around him and began moving him in the direction Kimber was running.

"I told you to wait at the stables," Nick said. He could feel the coat around his shoulders, but his arms didn't know there was anything on them at all.

"Zeke pulled the ASE up on his mobile. When I saw you out here without a coat, I couldn't just sit and watch. Frostbite happens fast at temps like these."

Both of them were moving forward together. Kimber was almost out of sight. He was running straight for Mrs. Claus. A pang of worry prodded at Nick. He had no idea what Kimber might be capable of, but when you're willing to go against your country, you're probably willing to hurt someone you don't know in order to get what you want.

14

"We've gotta hurry," Nick said through labored breath. Though he said it to Brooke, he was really talking to himself. She was the one pulling him along. He just couldn't get his legs moving. The outsides of his pants were packed with snow, accelerating the stiffness he was experiencing.

"I'll go ahead if you can't run," Brooke said.

"No." It was time for Nick to dial into his training. The pain was mental—all in his head. The stiffness was something he could overcome with movement. He gritted his teeth, lowered his head, and pushed forward. "He's heading straight for the Claus house. Mary will be in there alone. No telling what he might do to try to get out of this."

"Then stop yapping and get moving, soldier."

Nick looked up. "What?"

"I don't know, isn't that what an instructor might say?" Brooke shook her head. "Never mind. Let's just go!"

With Brooke's help, Nick was able to move faster. He could just make out Kimber's shadow as he turned right down a side street.

"If you were a better shot, we wouldn't be chasing," Nick said.

"And if I hadn't at least tried, you'd probably be dead."

Nick wanted to make another smartass remark—it was just who he was—but she might very well have been right. Without full use of his arms, Kimber probably would have eventually beat Nick to death.

Brooke's cell phone began to ring. "Where did he go?"

Brooke continued to impress Nick. She must have given Zeke her number before she came after them and told him to update her as he watched the ASE.

Brooke looked at Nick in horror. Though he couldn't hear Zeke, he knew by the look on her face that Kimber had gone to Mrs. Claus' house. It would be the natural thing to do on this street. The house was separated from everything else. It would have looked like a beacon to Kimber just sitting there at the end of the lane.

"Can you warn Mrs. Claus?" A pause. "Shit. Okay, we're going in." Brooke put the phone back in her pocket and looked at Nick. "Zeke tried to call Mrs. Claus, but she didn't answer. Probably asleep."

"Nice work, Brooke. But it's best I take it from here. I'm getting the feeling back in my arms." It was mostly true. Though his ability to move was still negligible, he was feeling tingles and pinpricks on the back of his arms.

"No chance. You dragged me up here, I'm not going to stand by while a national icon gets hurt, or worse, by a rogue CIA agent."

Nick's legs were beginning to loosen, though he still couldn't really feel the gun in his hand. He actually had to look down to make sure it was still there. Not good when you are going up against a tactical elite. But with Brooke alongside him, the advantage tipped in Nick's favor. As long as Kimber didn't make it to Mrs. Claus.

The two of them turned down the street and headed straight for the Claus home. It looked as if it were made out of gingerbread, complete with the picturesque snow-covered roof and glowing colored lights draped across its front. There was no sign of Kimber. But that was no surprise. Here in Santa's village, they didn't lock their doors. Never had a need to. Not until "Saint Nick" came to town—bringing his baggage of bad guys right along with him.

That was when they heard the scream.

Kimber had made it to Mary.

Nick exchanged a look with Brooke as they moved toward the front door. Nick was no longer running with Brooke's assistance, and he moved his gun hand to his mouth and continuously huffed hot air over it in an attempt to gain more feeling. It was getting better. The warmth inside the house when they walked through the door seemed to immediately help bring all of his senses back around. It was either that or the adrenaline. Probably the adrenaline, because it was flowing steadily at that point.

Brooke shut the door behind them. Nick knew Mrs. Claus' room was upstairs. For the first couple of weeks after he'd been first brought to the NP via dead Santa and his vigilant reindeer, Nick slept on the couch. It was like living at home with his parents (if they'd ever lived together), so it was nice. Mary treated him like a son—treatment he hadn't had in more than twenty-five years from his grandmother. His mom left when he was a kid, so the only warm childlike experiences he had were those few trips his drill sergeant dad had let him take to his grandparents' house.

The Claus house was quiet. Inside, it smelled of fresh

baked bread and an extinguished wood-burning fire. It was dark in the foyer, but what little light seeped in from the streetlamp outside showed that the bottom floor looked like Christmas had thrown up all over it. Ornaments, figurines, garland, tinsel—the whole nine yards. Nick held his arm out toward Brooke, motioning that they were going upstairs, but to stay behind him. Brooke nodded and fell in.

"Kimber. I know you're in here. Let's just talk this out." Nick waited for a response as he walked gingerly up, one slow step at a time. His gun up and ready. "There's no way out of this that doesn't end in you dead on the floor if you hurt Mary. Can we at least agree on that?" Another pause. "Let her go, and I won't kill you."

Finally, just as Nick was cresting the stairs, Kimber responded. "The way I see it, Nick, you're in no position to be making demands. Why don't you tell him, Mary?"

"Nick!" her voice came from what sounded like the far end of the hall. They were still in her bedroom. "He has a gun. Just do what he says!"

Nick's visceral reaction to hearing the fear in Mary's voice was to hang his head. He was disappointed in himself.

"It's okay, Mary. He's not gonna hurt you. He's in enough trouble as it is."

Then he heard Kimber laugh. More of a scoff really—straight from the gut. "That's why you're going to do exactly what I tell you, because I'm fried either way. The US doesn't take treason too lightly."

"Seems you should have thought of that before you decided to aid a terrorist."

Mary squealed in pain.

"I went easy on her with that one, Nick. Make another smartass remark and I'll really hurt her."

Nick could hear Mary begin to cry. He hated to admit it, Kimber had the upper hand, and Nick was going to have to give him what he wanted. As painful as that might be to do.

15

EVEN IN ALL THE COMMOTION, INTENSITY, AND HEAVINESS OF the moment, it wasn't lost on Nick that this was the most insane combat situation he'd ever been in. And he'd been in some crazy ones. Once in Afghanistan, he and three of his men had been pinned down, caught in a fire sack, enemy coming down on them from all sides. While that was certainly a lot more dangerous, it was still nowhere near as nuts as this. Here he was at the North Pole, Santa's reindeer at his beck and call, an elf working by his side every day, an FBI agent tagging along to help him follow protocol, and now a rogue CIA agent holding Mrs. Claus hostage in her very own home. Bonkers.

Now that they had been in the house for a minute, and he still had his coat on, his arms were beginning to feel normal again. But that didn't help the situation. As bad as it was in the house, the biggest problem with all of it was that if he didn't hurry, a terrorist was going to pull off an attack on American soil. Nick had to turn things around—fast.

"Okay, Kimber. You're right. I'm in no position to be

making demands. Don't hurt Mary. She has nothing to do with any of this. What is it that you really want?"

Nick eased up the last step. It was so quiet in that house —in that entire village—that the groan of the step could have been heard for a block away.

"You take another step and it won't matter to you what I want. You'll be too busy mopping Mrs. Santa up off the floor."

"Okay," Nick said. He stopped moving and leaned his back against the hallway wall as he pointed his gun toward Mary's room. "But let's cut the shit, all right, Agent Kimber?"

Nick had been thinking about what happened back at the house outside of London a lot while they were combing through the ASE earlier. Kimber had waited an awfully long time to move in once he got the all clear. When you have a window to take someone out—a "verified" window of time—you don't waste a second of it. Kimber had taken too long, and now that Nick knew Kimber was working for Nasir, it started to seem like Nick had been the one walking into the trap.

"Okay, Nick. I agree. Let's cut the shit. I want the cloaking device, and a ride on the reindeer train to wherever I want to go."

That was when it hit Nick that he had gone about all of this vigilante Santa thing exactly the wrong way. He should have never gone to the CIA. As a soldier, you get used to running every decision up the ranks. You don't move without being told to move. That was what drove Nick to think he should go through the CIA before he started fighting for his country with his new weapons. He could see now that was a mistake. The abilities Santa left Nick were too much for someone bad not to want. Now he was going to have to figure out how to correct his mistake now that the cat was already out of the bag.

"I didn't hear a *sir, yes sir!* soldier," Kimber mocked. "Follow orders, grunt. Or I'll shoot the old lady."

Nick knew he wouldn't shoot Mary. If he did, he'd never make it out of the North Pole alive. But that didn't mean he wouldn't hurt her. He wondered if there was a way to shut the cloaking device off from here if he let Kimber have it. That was something he and Zeke had never covered.

"Nick?" Brooke whispered.

"I can't let you have the cloaking device, Kimber," Nick said. "But I will give you a ride to anywhere you want to go. If you let Mary go, you have my word on that."

Kimber laughed, then stepped out into the hallway. He was holding Mrs. Claus in front of him with his right arm. His left hand had a gun to her head. "Yeah, right. And the entire time you'll follow me with the Seeing device. Listen, I'm not asking. I'm telling you to get me the cloaking device, or she's dead. Nick, you're not dealing with a small-time criminal here. I'm CIA. I'm already three steps ahead of you."

Nick hoped that Kimber continued to think that way. That he was smarter than Nick. It would make him complacent, and that would result in a mistake. He needed to play into that.

"You're right, Kimber. Just take the gun from Mary's head, and I'll get you the device. It's back in the warehouse."

"You can't let him have that," Brooke said. "Nasir can't get his hands on it. You know—"

"Brooke, let me handle this."

"Nick, he can't—"

"Brooke!" Nick shouted.

"I would listen to him, Brooke," Kimber said. "We'll

follow you to the warehouse. We're all going together."
Kimber shuffled Mary in front of him while keeping the
gun at her back.

Nick didn't speak. He backed his way down the stairs,
then out the door. Kimber followed with Mrs. Claus, using
her as a shield between them—never letting his gun down.
Mrs. Claus was crying. Nick was searching for a way to end
this without her getting hurt, and without Kimber flying off
to Nasir with a device to make him invisible. Though her
timing was poor, Brooke was right about what she said on
the stairs. Nasir could not get his hands on something that
powerful.

The cold walk was a long one. Nick had to shout
several times for the elves to go back inside. They were
gathering along the streets to see the horror that was
disrupting their utopia. The wind blew down the street,
freezing everyone even further. That was when a warming
thought crossed Nick's mind. Though he was disappointed
he hadn't remembered earlier, he was happy he had
before they made it to the warehouse. There were two
cloaking fobs. There was one back at the warehouse at the
ASE station. Normally that was where he put his when he
came back in from using it. But he remembered that this
time he'd never taken it out of his coat. The coat that
Brooke had brought to him after he'd forgotten it when he
ran out after Kimber. The freezing cold had definitely
affected his ability to think, but hopefully it didn't cost
them.

The cloaking fob was in his pocket, which was great. But
if he didn't use it at just the right moment, Kimber would
start shooting people until Nick reappeared. This was going
to be tricky. But it might actually work out far better now
instead of back inside Mary's house.

However, Nick might just have to let Kimber get away with the cloaking device after all.

16

MERCIFULLY, THE WALK BACK TO WAREHOUSE Z ENDED, AND Nick pushed inside. His ears were burning from the frozen wind that had been blustering through the village. On the way over, Nick had Zeke ready the sleigh as Kimber had requested. He would be bringing it to the warehouse any minute.

"No funny moves, Nick. Get the device and give it to me." Kimber was still holding onto Mrs. Claus. She had resigned herself to the fact that there was nothing she could do, so she had stopped crying.

Nick did exactly what Kimber asked and walked over to the ASE. The fob was hanging from a nail just to the right of the desk. Nick picked it up and held it high to show Kimber he wasn't going to try anything *funny*.

"Nick, for the last time, you can't just give him that," Brooke said. Her voice was pleading. She knew how much something like this would mean to a terrorist. If they were able to replicate it, all the enemies of state could execute their attacks unseen. A terrifying thought.

Nick didn't respond. He walked the fob over to Kimber

and handed it to him.

"Maybe you aren't so dumb after all," Kimber said.

"Nick, what are you doing?" Brooke tried again.

Kimber spoke instead. "He knows when he's been bested." Then to Nick, "Where's my ride?"

"It will be here any second. Now let Mary go."

"She's coming with me."

Although Nick had a plan, the thought of Mary being kept in this dangerous situation any longer made him sick. She was too kind and fragile for this. "Just leave her out of this, Kimber. Take me instead."

"How noble. Now put your gun on the table. You too, Brooke."

Once again, Nick did as asked. Brooke was incensed. "Nick? What are you doing? You can't just let him go with her *and* have the cloaking device!"

Nick had to play this all the way through. He looked at Brooke. "What do you want me to do? He got the jump on us when he found Mary. I can't let him hurt her."

"What do you think he'll do with her when he gets where he's going?"

"Seems like you should have maybe let her plan your mission," Kimber said. "She's smarter than you. In fact, I don't want her giving you any ideas."

Kimber raised his gun, pointing it right at Brooke. The fear on her face was enough to rattle anyone. Nick had seen plenty of terrified expressions during his years in combat scenarios, but this one still had an effect on him. As Nick reached for his gun, the door to the warehouse opened and Kimber pulled Mary close as he swung his gun toward the door. It was Zeke.

"Don't shoot! I have the sleigh!"

Kimber turned the gun back towards Nick, so Nick

froze. Unfortunately, Brooke did not. Before Nick could stop her, she was on Kimber. But she underestimated his skill. Kimber shucked Mary to the side, and caught an under-hook by getting his right arm beneath Brooke's left armpit. Using defensive Jiu Jitsu, he sprawled out, landing on top of her, and fired a warning shot at the table Nick's gun was sitting on. Nick's hand recoiled, and Brooke was struggling for air as she lay beneath Kimber. Nick took note of Kimber's abilities. Now he knew for certain he was the one that had been set up––it was clear to Nick that a man this skilled wouldn't have waited to go in that house alone. He'd been waiting for Nick. Kimber looked as though he would have been able to best all seven of the mostly untrained men back in London. Agent Andrews had led Nick right into a trap. All the while being dangled by the puppet master—Nasir Samara.

"Where did you find this one, Nick? She's got more heart than you." Kimber picked himself up, then pulled Brooke up by her ponytail. "I think I'll take her with me instead."

Brooke looked terrified. She was fully aware of what happened to hostages once they were taken to a second location. She also didn't understand that Nick actually had a plan. She had put herself in danger for no reason, though he couldn't help but admire her bravery. She would have made a hell of an Army Ranger. Unfortunately, there was nothing Nick could do at the moment, but let her be afraid. He hated that she was in Kimber's grip, but at least Mary wasn't. When Nick tagged along, it would be much easier to not have to worry about Mary's fragility. Even though Nick knew he wasn't just going to let Kimber take Brooke, it chewed him up to see Brooke think that he would.

"Honestly, Nick. I'm disappointed," Kimber said. "No

wonder they'd all but kicked you out of the Army before Santa came along and saved you. Whatever it is that made you hard enough to be a Ranger, it sure as hell is gone now. Delivering presents and eating cookies sounds like a good gig for you going forward. Good luck with it."

Kimber backed away toward the door, never taking his eyes off of Nick. "If this door opens before I'm on my way, I'll kill her, and you."

Nick felt something turn over in his brain when Kimber said he would kill him. *Why hadn't he already?* If roles were reversed, Nick would never let Kimber live to hunt him down. There must have been a bigger plan in place. One that they had to have Nick for. But they knew without the sleigh that Nick would be stuck here without a way to get to anyone. Regardless, he had to stick with his plan. Even more so now.

"It will be okay, Brooke. I'll find you," Nick said.

"Too late for hero talk, Nicky," Kimber said.

Brooke didn't even look Nick's way.

"Go pick up their guns and bring them to me," Kimber said to Zeke.

Zeke did as he was told. He too looked disappointed that Nick wasn't doing more.

Oh ye of little faith, Nick thought.

"Now, open the door, little man. Walk us out and show me how to drive this thing."

Zeke looked at Nick one last time. So did Brooke. Nick simply nodded for Zeke to do what Kimber said. Zeke hung his head and opened the door.

Nick readied himself for when the door shut. Kimber's skills had surprised Nick, but he had his own bag of tricks he'd learned over the years. And it was just about time to show them off.

17

"MARY, GET BACK TO THE HOUSE AND GET SOME REST." NICK picked up his phone and his gun, ready to press the button on the fob to go invisible. Time to make use of Santa's tricks. "I'm sorry I brought this here. It won't happen again."

"Just don't let him hurt that woman, Nick. That one's special."

Nick disappeared and moved past the gadgets Zeke had strewn about the middle of the warehouse to the back door on the opposite side. He moved quickly toward the far end of the outside of the building, the cold biting at his face. He hurried to the corner and looked around it. He saw Zeke pointing out some things that Kimber would need to know as he stood on the step above the skis of the sleigh. Nick looked behind him. His footprints followed him in the snow from the back door. He looked down and saw his own arms. Then he checked the fob to make sure the cloak was enabled. Green meant go, and the dot was glowing green just above the engage button. He was still getting used to this thing himself.

Zeke stepped down from the sleigh, then all of a

sudden, he was standing there alone. Kimber had hit the cloaking button on the sleigh and gone invisible. Nick sprinted for the now empty space beside Zeke. Under the lights that were shining down from the top of the warehouse, he could faintly see sleigh tracks forming in the snow, and they were beginning to move away from him.

Time to kick it in gear. Nick sprinted forward.

The first time he witnessed this phenomenon of the cloaking device, it had blown his mind. Jack had showed him how Santa managed to go unnoticed to houses all across the world. It had been Nick's first question. He still didn't understand how something so big could move without being seen or heard. But then again, he didn't understand how he could FaceTime his mother in Ashland, Kentucky, all the way from the Iraq desert either. The explanation Jack gave for how the cloak worked—something about the distortion of all atmospheric waves—was hardly helpful. Now, all that mattered was that the invisible sleigh didn't get away before he could hitch a ride. But it was beginning to move fast.

Nick stepped up the pace as he ran past Zeke. He was gaining on the end of the moving ski indentions in the snow. Just as he was about to catch it, they sped up. He knew the reindeer were pulling for takeoff. He reached forward for the back rail of the sled, but came up empty. The tracks moved away even faster. Then he remembered how when you were inside the cloak, you could only really tell you were invisible by the green light on the fob. In the sleigh's case, there was a green light above the cloak button on the dash beneath the reins.

Nick reached in his pocket and hit the second button on the black fob. Out of nowhere, the sleigh and the reindeer appeared, along with the back of Kimber and Brooke's heads. What also was now noticeable was that the three front reindeer were already off the ground. It was now or never. Nick drove the ball of his right foot down into the snow and leaped forward. As he dove through the air, he pocketed the fob and reached out with both hands. His left hand caught a good grip, but his right hand slipped. At the same time, the ground began to get farther away beneath him.

The sleigh's rail was wet with snow, and as it rose into the clouds, Nick nearly gave away his position with a shout as his hand slipped and he was forced to grab the ski below him with his right hand. As that hand began to slip, he pulled his legs up, wrapped them around the ski, and hugged it like a monkey on a wobbly branch. The air was even colder as the wind whipped by. He didn't dare look down. Instead, he took a deep breath, and felt for the foot grip above him where you step up on the back seat of the sleigh. He needed to find it before the sleigh went into its warp. Another thing Nick didn't understand. When it was time, the sleigh seemingly slipped through the fabric of time. Jack's explanation of that was much like the one for the cloaking device. Something about augmenting atmospheric waves. Nick's brain had shut off.

His brain needed to do the opposite at the moment. Finally, he was able to reach up enough to get a solid grip on the rubber-like floor of the sleigh's second row. Just as he was feeling the intense pull of the warp, he yanked himself into the back seat, and lay on his side. He reengaged the cloak with his fob and took a moment to catch his breath as the hot air blew from the vents at the bottom of the seat in front of him. He had no idea where they were going, but what he did know was that Kimber wasn't going to like what happened when they got there.

18

WHEN THE SLEIGH SLOWED FROM ITS WARP, IT DIDN'T TAKE long for Nick to recognize where they were. The point of the Washington Monument was reaching for the blue sky above, and the water of the reflecting pool shimmered beneath it. Kimber had a lot of nerve coming to the United States' capitol with treason leaking from his soul. Nick didn't know why, but the very thought of Kimber's audacity made his blood boil. Nick figured it just must be the patriot so engrained in him that made him so angry. He couldn't wait to take this guy down. Painfully, he would have to wait a little while longer. He needed to know where Nasir was going to be. Patience would be the only way through that dark tunnel.

"Why are you doing this?" Nick heard Brooke ask Kimber in the front seat. "Why would you turn your back on your own country?"

Kimber looked at her. "You are just as clueless as all the other Americans, aren't you? I would think being with the FBI you would know better. They don't care about us when we're out in the field. We're just pawns in their War Machine chess game."

"And you think Nasir Samara gives a damn about you? You can't be serious."

Nick would never have told Brooke, but he was really beginning to like her. He'd never met a woman with such gumption.

"This isn't about whether I think Samara cares about me. It's about teaching the CIA a lesson in not caring about their agents."

"Really? You didn't know the job description before you signed up? Sounds like it's your fault, because I know exactly how they operate, and I don't even work for them."

Kimber backhanded Brooke in the face. Her head snapped around far enough that Nick could see both her eyes. Nick's hands were on their way to wrapping around Kimber's throat when the sleigh made a hard right and tilted down toward the ground. Brooke didn't respond to the slap. She simply wiped the blood that trickled from her mouth and kept her eyes forward. Nick hadn't had any plans to actually kill Agent Kimber. That might have just changed.

As Nick was seething in the backseat, the sleigh was moving down toward a neighborhood somewhere about a mile from the White House. Nick didn't know much about D.C., but it didn't matter. He had texted Zeke to send his location via the Find My iPhone app to Jim Calipari. As much as he hated for it to be Jim, the stealer of his college crush and the man he'd just gone head to head with in a put-down match just yesterday at the LA jail, he was the only person in power Nick could trust. He couldn't send any of this information to the CIA. Nick had already run into two rogue agents. What was to say the director herself wouldn't be compromised as well? He didn't know how far up Nasir had been able to penetrate.

Nick didn't like Jim. But he knew Jim liked Brooke. When Zeke's message made it to Jim, telling about how Kimber had taken Brooke hostage, Nick knew he would use whatever powers he had at the FBI to help. Nick only hoped he wouldn't need it. Not here with Kimber at least. The attack that Nasir Samara was planning might be a completely different story.

The sun was just coming up over the capitol, so it was quiet around the street they landed on. The neighborhood was full of townhomes, and all of them were covered in a light snow and a smattering of festive decorations. Kimber hoisted Brooke to her feet as he held his gun to her back.

"Don't make any sounds. I will shut you up if I have to."

Brooke didn't respond. She just let Kimber lead her to the edge of the sleigh where he stopped abruptly. He took a second to look around, seemingly to see if anyone were watching, and a sly smile grew across his smug face. He reached into his pocket, then he and Brooke disappeared. The cloaking device worked to cloak anyone in a one foot radius of the fob. That's why Brooke went invisible with him. Zeke must have explained this to Kimber because before they were cloaked, Kimber had wrapped his arm around Brooke's waist and pulled her close.

There was just enough snow on the ground to see Brooke's footprint as she stepped down from the sleigh. Kimber's immediately followed. No sound came from them; not even the squeak of a shoe. The cloaking device continued to blow Nick's mind. He stepped down behind them and followed the appearing footsteps to the front door of the red-brick townhome. A man wearing a black ski mask opened the door for them—probably yet another corrupt agent—and Kimber and Brooke reappeared. Nick understood right then that Kimber had texted ahead and told this agent to wear a mask. Kimber hadn't forgotten the ASE could see all if it dialed in. The masked agent jumped back in shock when Kimber came out of nowhere. Nick couldn't see his facial expression, but his body language said it all.

"Pretty cool, right?" Kimber said. Then both of them stepped inside.

"Unreal," the agent at the door responded.

The agent was still bewildered, and that gave Nick the opportunity to rush through the door as the agent marveled at The Amazing Kimber and his beautiful blonde assistant. Nick's combat boots squeaked loudly against the tile floor as he stopped himself from running into Kimber's back. It was absolutely mind busting that they couldn't hear it— pure magic—and Nick danced quickly around the two agents before the man at the door ran into him from behind. He could see a bit of mud streak from his shoes so he stopped in his tracks and took them off. He wasn't going to let residue be the thing that blew his cover.

The first floor of the townhome looked completely normal upon entering. Ten-foot ceilings, open floor concept, the kitchen to the left, open to the living room to the right. That was where the normalcy ended. Instead of a couch and a TV, there were workstations set up. Four desks with two monitors atop each of them, and a man sitting at three of the four of them. All three of them wore masks, and they were all looking at Agent Kimber and Brooke, which was freaking Nick out, because to do so, they were looking straight through him. Nick walked over to the far right wall to take in the scene.

Never in the history of US intelligence, or any other

agency throughout the world, could an agent actually be a fly on the wall. It was one of the most worn-out cliché statements in combat—wishing you could be a fly on the wall during an enemy's meeting. Now, there Nick stood, ready to take it all in; absolutely no one the wiser.

Kimber pushed Brooke along and sat her in a seat at the small dining table that separated the kitchen from the living room.

"This is Brooke, she's FBI. She won't be staying with us long. And in case you didn't notice, I got the cloaking device. It's actually real."

Kimber pulled the fob from his pocket, pressed the button, on-off, on-off, appearing and reappearing like he was a hologram. The men in the room marveled.

"All right, enough fun," Kimber said as he put away the fob. "Time to get down to business. Has he arrived yet?"

"Twenty minutes ago," a masked man at the first computer station in the room answered.

Nick's adrenaline spiked a bit. If they were talking about Nasir, Nick was actually going to get a chance to take him down himself. It would be a Ranger's dream to take down any terrorist leader, but for Nick, it meant so much more. Six years ago, he led a team into Nasir's camp in Afghanistan. Just as Nasir had inside information this time from Kimber and Andrews, he'd had inside information that a team of Ranger's were moving in. And it cost Nick seven of his twelve-man team. Including his closest friend in the world, Ricky Thompson. Worst of all was that Nasir wasn't even there. A video surfaced a day later of his ugly mug taking credit for killing so many of the elite US combat soldiers. Much like Santa––Nick supposed—Nick had put Nasir's name on a list. It wasn't the naughty list, of course, but if the list did have a name, the word *kill* would be somewhere in it.

"Okay, is everything set? You let him know I am here? Because I messaged him as I was leaving the North Pole, but haven't heard back from him." Kimber said.

"Everything is ready to go."

"All right, don't say another word. Shut this down and move out. This place has served its purpose, but now it is burned."

19

NICK LOOKED ON FROM THE WALL OF THE TOWNHOME TURNED intelligence center—invisible as the wind. He was ready to take them all out, but he wanted to get as much information as he could about the attack Nasir was planning. It could mean saving hundreds of lives. If Kimber was dumb enough to talk about it. Either way, Nick was ready. He already had his finger wrapped around his Beretta's trigger as he held it down by his side.

"What do you mean this place is burned?" the masked man at the computer said to Kimber as he stood. "How? Were you followed?"

"Yes, but not in the way you think. They can see everything. That's the reason you have masks, so they won't have your identities if something goes wrong. This Nick, he might be dialed into the all-seeing device and watching right now. That's why we are leaving right now to head back to the North Pole to take every scrap of technology they have. With the cloaking device, and the All-Seeing Eye, we won't need guys like Nasir Samara anymore. Every rich guy in need of a mercenary crew will be beating down our doors. That is, of course, if we don't sell this stuff to the highest bidder. It could be worth billions."

"We're not going to give the device to Nasir?" the man in the mask asked.

"Didn't you hear what I said? It's worth billions. And it's unguarded. The five of us here can easily go and take it now."

"But you didn't kill the Army Ranger while you were there? We'll have to deal with him."

"Nasir said we needed someone to show us how it all worked, that's why he wanted him alive. I could easily have killed him, but I wasn't sure about taking the technology for ourselves yet."

"Okay, what changed your mind? How do you know this will work?"

"The ride here changed my mind. As silly as it sounds we can be anywhere we want in minutes with this *sleigh*. Undetected. The sky is literally the limit. This place at the North Pole is so remote, they'll never find us. And by the time they maybe could, we'll have it set up like a fortress."

Nick couldn't believe what he was hearing. Kimber had made a lot of changes in his plan since seeing how the ASE worked. Nick had done the same when he saw it, but he wanted to use it for good. Kimber obviously had other intentions, and Nick had to end things right then and there. Kimber's next words made him pause.

"What about Nasir? Won't he come after us?"

"Just shut everything down here. I'll take care of Nasir when he gets here."

Kimber's masked agent let out a satisfied laugh.

Nick wanted to be the one waiting for Nasir, and he couldn't let Kimber take a single step outside this house. Nick couldn't put the North Pole, and more importantly, all of its technology at risk for another second. He had to end this threat right here, right now.

He didn't get the chance.

Before the sound of the suppressed weapon registered, the back of Kimber's head disappeared. There was a new masked man standing at the entrance to the back hallway. Several more shots from his suppressed gun popped off, but Nick didn't see who they hit. He raised his Beretta and shot the masked man who'd just killed Kimber three times in his chest. Then it was pure chaos.

Brooke's scream echoed above it all as she dove under the table she'd been sitting beside. The front door burst inward, and several more men came running in. Nick looked to his left. Two of Kimber's men were still alive, and the unsuppressed gunshots blasted into the air. Nick and Brooke were caught in the crossfire. He dove to the ground and Army-crawled toward the table Brooke was hiding under. He grabbed her arm, cloaking her, and the fear on her face shifted to a terrified look of relief. He pulled his legs under himself as he covered her with his body. There was nothing he could do but wait. He couldn't risk her getting hit. He'd already put her in enough danger.

The gunfire continued for a few more seconds until the rest of Kimber's team was down. Nick pulled his head back far enough from Brooke so that she could see his face. Then he mouthed the words *stay down*. She shook her head no and grabbed at him to stay. Before Nick could make his move, he looked over her shoulder and saw a man with goggles over his eyes, bent down, pointing his gun at Brooke's back.

In a Middle Eastern accent, the man said, "Drop the gun, *Santa*, or I'll blow the back of her head through the front of yours."

Nick could tell the goggles were infrared. Though the man holding the gun couldn't see Brooke and Nick, Nick knew he was picking up their shapes through thermal imaging. Nick had no choice, he had to drop the gun, because there were five other men in the room now, all pointing their guns in his direction. Adding insult to injury, Nick knew this was Nasir Samara: the man who murdered half his team—his brothers—six years ago, and there was nothing he could do about it.

"All right. Don't shoot." Nick laid his gun on the hardwood floor and pushed it out from under the table.

"Now, in slow movements, turn off the cloaking device."

Nick's mind was racing, searching for a way out. His ace in the hole was that Nasir not only didn't know how to work any of the technology, which was why he needed Nick. Nasir also didn't know how to get the sleigh to take him back to the North Pole. Normally, Nasir wouldn't even have known where the sleigh was, but his infrareds couldn't miss eight warm-blooded reindeer standing out on the street on a cold winter day. He didn't have many options, but the one thing he could do was ensure that Nasir didn't get on the sleigh. Not immediately anyway.

Nick reached into his pocket and felt the fob in his hand. He thumbed the front of it, feeling the top button, which turned his cloaking device on and off. He pressed it, hoping that would make Nasir lift his infrared goggles for a moment, giving Nick time to press the second button while his goggles were off, so he wouldn't see the sleigh leave the street.

"All right, I did what you asked. Now let her go."

Nick looked over Brooke's shoulder and watched Nasir lift the goggles. It was the first time he'd looked the monster that ambushed his team in the eyes. He had to swallow the rage that moved like a tidal wave over his body. It was a win that Nasir removed the goggles. He knew there might not be another win for a while, so he had to take advantage of this one.

"Now the fob," Nasir said. "Toss it over to me."

As Nasir spoke, Nick ran his thumb down to the second button. On a car, this would be considered the panic button. Jack had explained that sometimes Santa would have to move the sleigh before he could get back to it. He said that Santa couldn't always land on a roof, and sometimes something would be about to walk into the sleigh while it was cloaked so he had to put this button on the fob for those instances. When pressed, the reindeer would feel a vibration on their harnesses. They'd been trained that this meant for them to go back to the stables at the North Pole. When Santa pressed the button again, they would come back to the location of the fob.

Nick hadn't actually seen this happen. He'd never pressed that button to make them leave. All he could do was press and hope, and that was what he did. He had to hold it for three seconds—a safety against an accidental press. You had to hold it three seconds to bring them back as well.

"The fob!" Nasir shouted.

Nick held it for an extra second, just to be certain, then tossed the fob from under the table, and it slid over to Nasir's feet. That was it, Nick was officially out of moves. Now he and Brooke were at the mercy of a terrorist. Nick knew what that meant for him. An Army Ranger and American patriot like him would most certainly end up on a video with his head being removed. What he didn't know, and what he had to fight against now, is what they might do to Brooke.

20

Nasir bent down and picked up the cloaking fob.

"Stand the two of them up," Nasir ordered his men.

Two men dressed in black walked around the table and yanked Nick and Brooke to their feet.

"Your first test, Mr. Santa," Nasir smirked.

A flame of adrenaline sparked inside Nick. He felt like a pit bull on a leash, just waiting to get the chance to attack. But there was nothing he could do. Yet.

"How does it work?" Nasir said. "Lie to me, and she gets hurt. I don't have much time, so don't play games."

Nick decided it was best to give him what he wanted. "Okay, but to get the full effect, you should stand in front of a mirror."

"So I can see myself disappear," Nasir said.

"That is if you even have a reflection."

Nasir shot Nick a look. Nick could tell Nasir didn't get the vampire joke.

There was a mirror behind Nick at the end of the dining room table. Nasir walked over and stood in front of it. Nasir could see himself from the waist up. Nick could see even better now that he was an ugly son of a bitch. His olive-yellow skin was his best feature. His dark, deep set eyes were hideous, and the ski-slope disguised as a nose was just disgusting.

"Press the top button," Nick said. "Anything within a foot of you will go invisible."

Nasir was almost close enough to reach out and touch. Nick knew he could get to Nasir and kill him before his men could react. The problem was that it would leave Brooke completely exposed.

Nick watched as Nasir stood in the mirror, and he could tell he was getting frustrated.

"I told you not to lie to me. This button isn't working!"

At first Nick couldn't understand what the problem was. Then he remembered that they hadn't been able to find Nasir on the ASE. And the reason the cloaking device wasn't working for him right then was the same reason Nick and Zeke couldn't find him on the ASE.

"Turn off your jammer. Then it will work," Nick said.

A wry smile grew across Nasir's scraggily bearded face. He dug inside his pocket and tossed a small, black square object on the table. There was a short antenna jutting from the top of it. Nick had seen these many times before. It was a radio jammer. Just as Nick had suspected back in the warehouse.

Nasir turned back toward the mirror, then he disappeared. A second later, he reappeared, and he was laughing. There was astonishment in the room. It didn't matter what kind of dark soul you had, the invisibility cloak had the ability to bring the innocent child out in you.

Nasir pressed the button a couple more times. Disappearing and reappearing with delight. Then he put the fob in his pocket, and the resting bitch face that Nick assumed he always wore returned.

"Good, you passed." He looked at two of his men by the hallway. "Get the car ready. Two of you might be taking the woman."

Nick didn't like the word 'might'. He knew in terrorist speak that it meant she was going to die.

Nasir glanced down at the jammer on the table, still wearing that putrid little smirk. "Guess I won't be needing that anymore." Now Nasir's face was smug. His black ball cap was pulled down low, but Nick could still see the evil in his eyes. "Been carrying that around for a long time. I've figured for a while now that the US would come up with a way to illegally intrude on my right to privacy. This was always just a precaution. It pays to be meticulous."

Nick didn't give him the satisfaction of a reaction.

Nasir walked over and stood right in from of Nick. "All right. You are one for one. Now for test number two. If you pass this one, I'll let her live."

Nick knew he was about to ask about the second button on the fob. He couldn't tell him the truth about that one. But he was going to have to sound convincing in the lie. Nick nodded.

"The second button?"

Nick didn't hesitate. "A distress signal." Short and sweet.

Nasir laughed. Nick couldn't decide whether that was good or bad. When Nasir reached in the pocket of his black pants, pulled out a gun, and pointed it at Nick's head, he supposed then that it wasn't good. Nasir stopped laughing.

"Does it look like I have time for jokes? What is the button for?"

Nick had heard somewhere that if you are going to lie, commit to it. If he was going to die right here, he wasn't going to half ass it. "It's what I said, a distress signal, but not in the life or death way you are thinking."

No reaction from Nasir. But he did move his gun from Nick's head, over to Brooke's.

Nick continued, "They put it in place so that if Santa ever got stuck in a house or separated from the sleigh, he could press that button and it would relay his exact location. That's all. Nothing exciting."

This was obviously a lie, but Nick was hoping that the grain of truth in it would be convincing enough. While button two wasn't a distress signal, it did give the read of the fob's location when pressed. That was how the reindeer would make it back to Santa when he held down the button. Jack had also said that it didn't give off the GPS coordinates because the GPS somehow interfered with the cloaking device. You couldn't be cloaked and call for the sleigh. If you pressed and held the button, the cloak would shut off for ten seconds to show command back at the North Pole where Santa was.

"Why doesn't it always give off the GPS coordinates?" Nasir said, still holding his gun on Brooke.

Nick would have asked the same question. Nick gave the explanation about the cloak interference, leaving out the part about it sending the reindeer back.

Nasir pulled down his gun and put it away. "We must leave now. You two, take the woman. You know what to do with her. Santa, you're coming with me. I'm excited to see where I'll be spending most of my time from now on."

Nick knew he meant the North Pole. A terrorist's dream location. He also knew that he couldn't let Nasir's men take Brooke. No matter what. Because they were absolutely going to kill her.

"I'd love to take you to the North Pole, but you're a

desert man. You'll freeze to death up there. I don't want that on my conscience."

Nick had nothing else. He hoped by using sarcasm, Nasir might at least take a minute to beat the hell out of him. Maybe that could give Nick a window.

"I'm not worried about your conscience. Take me to the sleigh, right now, or I'll shoot her where she stands."

Nasir didn't go for it.

"I would if I could," Nick said. "But the sleigh isn't here, and I'll only tell you how to get it back here if you let her go."

Nasir went for that one. He took his pistol back out, took the barrel in his hand, and pistol-whipped Nick on the top of the head with the butt of the gun. Nick dropped to a knee. The sting of the blow wasn't pleasant, but Nasir maybe weighed a buck-thirty soaking wet, so it didn't do the damage to Nick that he knew Nasir had hoped.

"Lie to me again, and she's dead. I'm not threatening again. She means absolutely nothing to me!"

There was real anger in his voice now. Nick had to tread lightly.

"I know where the sleigh is, I saw it out front when I had the infrareds on. I just need you to fly it!"

"I'm telling you, it's not there. Look again. I haven't lied to you yet."

Nasir stepped away from Nick and walked over to the window that looked out over the road. Nick was hoping that the button to send the sleigh home had worked. If it was still there, he was going to have to risk everything to try to save Brooke from Nasir's wrath. The man that was holding Nick stood him up. Nick turned his head enough to watch Nasir. Nasir pulled the goggles back over the brim of his hat and down over his eyes. He immediately took them back off and threw them on the ground in anger. But before Nick could be happy about the sleigh being gone, and before Nasir could turn around to take his anger out on Nick, three black Ford Crown Vics came sliding into view, followed by a black van that had the glorious acronym 'S.W.A.T.' in big, white, bold letters down its side.

Jim had come through. Zeke had got him the message.

21

As soon as Nick read the letters S.W.A.T. on the black van, Nasir disappeared. He literally vanished into thin air. Nick already knew how powerful this technology was in the wrong hands, but watching a cornered terrorist—one of the most dangerous humans on Earth—be there one second and gone the next drove home just how disastrous it would be to let him get away as a ghost. Especially since they were only about a mile from the most powerful American on the planet—the President of the United States.

Nick had never been all that into politics. However, when your future missions overseas depend on the political climate at home, word gets around about certain things. One of the most discussed topics on any military base was the public feud between Nasir Samara and President Clark. Both had vowed to kill each other, and remembering that made Nick sick with worry that he didn't currently have eyes on Nasir.

Nick watched armed men step out of the van on the street. Then he spun into the man holding him so fast that the man couldn't hold his grip. Nick drove his forehead down on the man's nose and rammed his knee into the man's groin. He immediately kicked the man in the leg that was holding Brooke, driving his foot down into the side of the man's knee. The man shouted in pain as it caved in sideways, and collapsed to the floor. Nick grabbed Brooke by the collar of her coat and yanked her to the floor. Her momentum slid her underneath the dining room table, and finally, the other two men in the room caught up and began firing at Nick.

Nick dropped to the ground as bullets from a semi-automatic rifle pelted the wall, shattering the mirror behind him. He reached into the man's holster that he had just headbutted to unconsciousness. He pointed the gun to his left and shot the man on the ground with the busted knee as he was pulling a gun of his own. Next, he scooted on his knees over to and behind the far end of the dining room table. Nasir's men had not stopped shooting. Nick knew that the black cars, and SWAT, outside were because of the call he had Zeke make to Jim. He also knew that they would not enter this building while live rounds were still blasting. They wouldn't know who to shoot, and who not to. Nick had to get Brooke out of this himself. Then he had to get to Nasir. A sinking suspicion that he was heading straight for the White House needled at the back of Nick's brain.

That would have to wait.

Nick listened as the two men continued to fire on him. Bullets sprayed the table, the wall, and even the chair beside him. Then he heard the man on the left's magazine click empty, so Nick dove to his left and shot three times for the man's chest. Before he could watch him drop, Nick rolled back over, just dodging a string of bullets from the last man standing. Then that man's mag was empty too. Nick rose up to put an end to the situation, but before he could shoot, the man dove behind the island in the middle of the open kitchen. Nick heard him lock a fresh magazine in place.

He had to act fast.

The last roll he made on the floor put him beside Kimber's body. The image of Nasir disappearing flashed in his mind, spurring him to reach in Kimber's pocket for the second cloaking fob. When his hand found it, just as he hit the button and rolled into Brooke under the table, the man stood up in the kitchen and fired into the now empty looking room. Only a couple of shots in, the man stopped, most likely baffled by the absence of his target. Nick poked his torso above the table and shot the man twice, one round hit his chest, the other right in the neck.

Nick turned and saw the armed men had taken up position outside. He knew they had already surrounded the house by going around back as well.

"Brooke, I have to go after Nasir," he said as he pressed the button on the fob to uncloak himself.

Brooke stood up. She was breathing heavy. Nick was used to firefights, but it was clear that Brooke was not by the dazed look on her face. Nick stepped forward and took her face in his hands. "Brooke, get outside and tell them to lock down the White House. Make sure they get the President somewhere safe!"

Brooke snapped out of her trance. "You can't go after him. Let the FBI and Secret Service handle it."

Nick moved toward the hallway that led to the back of the house. He was certain this was the way Nasir had gone. "Brooke, they're not going to understand this cloaking device and how dangerous it is. How Nasir can just walk right through the front door of the White House and security won't even know it. Just make sure the President is secured, and make sure police, FBI, CIA, and whoever else you can, lock down the airports. Including the private planes. I've got to go."

"Okay. Just—be careful! I'll get on trying to find out where Nasir came into the country."

Nick nodded, hit the cloaking button, and turned down the hallway. As soon as he did, SWAT burst into the front and back doors. Nick sucked himself up against the wall as three men in full tactical gear raced by him, then he walked out the front door like a breeze through a window.

The first thing he did was jog a block down the street that ran behind the townhomes and hide behind a big inflatable Santa Claus lawn decoration. The irony wasn't lost on him as he uncloaked himself. He had to call Zeke and he couldn't do so while the device was active. It jammed the cell phone signal.

"Boss, you okay?"

"Zeke, is there a way to shut these cloaking devices down from command?"

Silence.

"Zeke!"

"I'm thinking. I've never thought about it. Never had a reason—"

"Zeke, the President of the United States is in trouble. The bad guy has the cloaking fob, and I need you to shut it off before he is able to find the president. You understand?"

Zeke replied lazily, "Well . . . I can take a look—"

"Zeke! This is life or death. I need you to work fast. Got it? Like if you're old pal Santa was delivering presents and was going to die if you couldn't shut down the device. That kind of fast."

Zeke's tone changed. "Okay, yeah! I'm on it!"

Nick was about to say something else, but hung up

instead when two agents came around the back of the townhome on his right. He pulled up the navigation app on his phone and typed in the walking directions to 1600 Pennsylvania Ave. He looked at the turn by turn, and he was less than a mile. When he rose to his feet to start running, something across the street stopped him in his tracks.

Nick cloaked himself, waited for a couple of cars to pass, then ran right over to the black SUV with the tailgate lifted wide open. Normally it wouldn't have mattered to him, but no one was around, and he remembered that Nasir had come in through the back of the townhome earlier. When he got to the back of the truck, whatever worry he had for the president a moment ago, it immediately turned into panic.

Sitting in the back of the SUV were three backpacks. Nick opened the one closeted to him and his fear was confirmed. It was a bomb. Nick realized that the entire plan of attack for Nasir's act of terror had been based solely on getting Nick to bring the cloaking technology right where Nasir wanted it. Where he could do the most damage. Nick had fallen right for it.

And now the entire White House was about to pay for it.

22

As he had countless other times in his life, Nick was heading straight toward danger when most would have been running from it. He'd had the thought on multiple occasions that he had to either be stupid or crazy to throw himself into the situations he had over the past two decades. He'd always come to the conclusion that he was probably a little bit of both. However, in this situation, he had just been plain stupid.

Instead of helping to keep his beloved country safe from monsters like Nasir Samara, he'd all but thrown the president to the unseeable wolves. He didn't think that the problem was that he had acted too fast; he just should have never gone to the CIA with what he had at the North Pole in the first place. That was the lesson he should have learned from the real Santa. Only let people believe or not believe that you exist, don't actually show them. Because that was when evil could find you too. Nick was beating himself up about it while he was still a quarter of a mile away, because once he made it to the White House, his focus would need to be at a hundred and ten percent.

Nick swerved onto Pennsylvania Avenue. The morning sun was strong, and blinding him through the windshield. He didn't have time to worry about the people that would see the driverless SUV that he was whipping toward the White House while cloaked in invisibility. And he wasn't going to have time to care what security thought when he crashed right through the gates. Because he would be a ghost on his way into the White House by the time they could get there to check it out.

Nick had only visited the White House once in his life. So he only had a vague recollection of what it looked like and how it was laid out. But that didn't really matter. He was hoping that he wouldn't have to even go inside. Of course, his hopes were resting in the hands of a half-crazy elf at the North Pole, but Zeke was a mad scientist when it came to weaponry, so Nick did his best to believe that Zeke would be able to remove Nasir's cloak. By Nick's estimation, he and Nasir should be getting to the president's home at about the same time. He just hoped he wouldn't be too late.

Nick could see the White House now in the distance. He was swerving in and out of morning traffic—even using the oncoming lane and the shoulder when he had to. He was so focused on what part of the security barrier he would crash through that he jumped when his cell phone rang.

"Zeke, give me the good news!" Nick swerved right, then all the way back left into oncoming traffic as he dodged the commuters.

"I can disable the cloak, but . . ." Zeke sounded unsure.

"But what, I don't have time to waste!"

"But it will disable yours too. That okay?"

The White House was just a block away now. Nick scanned the grounds and found a place in the fence to drive the SUV through. Then he found which path he would take to the entrance.

"Nick?"

"Count to thirty and shut them down. Make sure you put howdy-dos in between each number."

"Howdy what?"

"One-howdy-do." Nick swerved one last time and floored the gas pedal. "Two howdy-do, and so on. Got it?" he shouted. His adrenaline was pumping.

"Oh, yeah. Never heard anyone say it like—"

"Zeke!" Nick shouted as the SUV approached the gate that surrounded the White House. "Focus! As soon as the cloak goes down, find Nasir on the ASE and pipe it into my phone. Got it?"

"Got it."

Nick ended the call and slid the phone back inside his pocket just as the grill of the SUV slammed into the eight-foot-high, black wrought iron fence. The collision jarred him so hard that he slammed his forehead against the top of the steering wheel. The SUV barely made it through, but it was enough for Nick to move forward. He shook his head to clear the cobwebs. The front end of the SUV was hissing at him. It was unquestionably damaged beyond the ability to keep driving. He unbuckled his seatbelt, exited the truck, and started toward the White House. With a glance over his shoulder, he could already see security coming his way.

Good thing he was still invisible.

By Nick's count, he had about fifteen seconds before the cloak was removed. All he could hope was that Nasir had yet to be able to place the bomb. Nick was no explosives expert, but what was in those bags looked nasty enough to do some *serious* damage. Nasir wouldn't even have to be inside the White House for them to be catastrophic. Nick also didn't know if one or two bags were missing. If Nasir had been able to place two bombs, if Brooke hadn't been able to move word up the chain of command fast enough to get the president down in the PEOC, there was actually a good chance the POTUS could die today.

That thought spurred Nick into a jog. Ten seconds to go until he was just an unknown crazy that crashed himself into the White House fence. He made his way toward the left side. There were plenty of trees and brush there to give him cover while he scanned for Nasir.

With five seconds left, Nick ducked behind a row of trees. He heard some commotion on the street at the opposite side of the White House. Once again, the black van and the SWAT acronym in white was a hopeful sight. Especially with two more behind it, followed by a couple of camouflage Humvees. It meant that Brooke had been able to get word to the president. But that didn't mean he was safe. Nick still *had* to find this bomb, and he needed help.

Time should have passed for the cloak to be removed. He took a knee behind a tree and checked his fob. The light was red. He was now visible. Which meant Nasir was too. To be sure, he dialed Zeke.

"You're all good," Zeke answered.

"You mean I'm visible?"

"Oh yeah. Already found you on the ASE. Is that *the* White House?"

Nick ignored the question. "I need you to call Brooke, right now. Tell her there is one bomb bag, possibly two, and I need everyone to help me find it. I'd talk to them myself, but I just ran a truck through the gate. I'm pretty sure they'll take me down."

"Dialing her now."

"While you do that, bring up Nasir on the ASE. And send it to my phone. I've got to stop him!"

"Ahead of you. Just pulled him up. Nick, he's at the White House too. He just set some sort of timer on a machine. Not good."

"Gotta go. Call Brooke and get me some help. I've got a terrorist to catch."

Nick ended the call, swiped over on his phone, and pulled up the ASE app that would allow him to see what Zeke was seeing right there on his phone. He tapped the app and a little elf danced on the screen to signify loading. And it just kept dancing.

Nick looked up and saw that the SUV he'd crashed was swarmed with military and security personnel. Sirens were echoing across the city. A city that no doubt was going into lockdown mode. If it hadn't been Christmas Eve, Nick would never have made it here in time—*if* he had actually made it in time. Traffic on a normal Tuesday wouldn't have allowed it. And it wouldn't have allowed the extra armed men coming to help to get there so quickly either. He was at least thankful for that.

Finally, the elf stopped dancing, and Nick rose to his feet. Just in time to see Nasir running toward someone standing in a bunch of trees.

Nick felt a heavy blow on the back of his head before he could realize it was Nick himself that Nasir had been running toward. Later he would kick himself for relying too much on technology, and not the combat instincts he'd expertly honed over his twenty years in the Army. But right then, he couldn't kick himself for anything, because he was too busy falling to the ground—unconscious.

23

NICK JOLTED AWAKE. HE WAS LYING FACE DOWN BETWEEN TWO thorny bushes. Before he sat up, he checked his phone. There was a missed call from Brooke. He checked the clock––he hadn't been out long––only a few seconds had gone by as far as he could tell. As he pushed himself up to a crouch, he wondered why Nasir hadn't killed him. Then he realized it was actually smart that he hadn't. The blast of an unsuppressed gun would surely have gotten him caught. Nick must have been close when the cloak went away. Nasir must have seen him after he placed the bomb.

The bomb!

Brooke was calling him again, but he clicked to ignore it and quickly dialed Zeke.

"You're okay!"

"Zeke, where is the bomb Nasir was setting the timer on?"

Zeke didn't miss a beat. "Go to the wall of the White House across from you. About twenty feet down, the bag is nestled between two bushes."

He had only been twenty feet from Nasir. If Nick hadn't

been so worried about security seeing him, he would have spotted Nasir and been able to take him out. But there was no time to dwell on what couldn't be changed. Nick ran across the opening to the wall of the White House. Sure enough, there was the bag.

"Zeke, find Nasir and send his location to Brooke. I'll call you when I need you. Be on standby!"

Nick opened the bag, and sure enough, the clock was counting down. Only two minutes to go.

"I already have Nasir. Been following him since he knocked you out. He jumped the fence and used his gun to take a car. The big guys in the Army clothes like you wear almost got to him, but he drove away. Why don't they make that fence taller if that house is so important?"

Nick ignored the last question. He was busy scanning the area for the best place to throw the bag to ensure minimal damage.

"Never mind," Zeke said. "More important, he tossed another bag right after he knocked you out. It was strapped to his back."

Nick closed his eyes and recalled the image on his phone. He did remember Nasir having something on his back.

Zeke kept talking, "So you should probably disable that one and get to the next one before it blows up."

"You know something about how to disarm it, do ya?" Nick said sarcastically. He knew Zeke didn't know anything about bombs. He picked up the bag, and started running toward the back of the White House where he knew there was some kind of park. This early in the morning, it should be pretty empty.

"No," Zeke said. "I don't know anything about them, really. But when I was doing my countdown to shut down the cloak, I had the ASE keyed in on Nasir. As soon as the cloak shut off, I watched him type in the combination on the keypad."

Just as Zeke's words registered, two armed guards at the back of the White House spotted Nick and began shouting at him. They had him dead to rights. Nick had no choice but to freeze, because if they shot him like Nick knew they would, not only would the bomb in his hand go off, but so would the other one Nasir had been able to plant before he ran. And that would have a devastating amount of casualties.

"Nick, did you hear me?" Nick could hear Zeke, but couldn't respond. "I know how to stop it!"

Nick was relieved to hear Zeke say that, but he had to survive security before he could breathe easy. He held the bomb bag up in the air. "I have a bomb! It's on a timer!" He needed to get their attention, and with that, he certainly did. The two men stopped running toward him and raised their guns. They were only about thirty feet from him. "Just listen to me. I can shut it off, but I need you to let me do it. If you shoot me, a lot of people are going to die."

"Put the bag down and step away. Now!" the man on the left shouted.

"Listen to me!" Nick shouted back. "This bomb is going to explode in one minute! Don't shoot! I'm on your side!"

The men shouted at him again, but Nick didn't have time to heed their warnings. He dropped to a knee and opened up the bag. He was looking at an electronic keypad that was attached to the front of some sort of explosive. "What's the combination, Zeke!"

Again, Zeke didn't hesitate. "5, 9, 3,7, and 5. Then push the red button below the numbers."

"Step away from the bag, right now, or we'll shoot!" the man screamed.

There was now a helicopter overhead. If he didn't hurry, Nick knew they were going to take him out. If Nick were on their side of this, he would have already shot. Good thing he wasn't. The timer was at thirty seconds.

"Just wait!" Nick shouted. "I'm shutting it down!"

In his peripheral vision, Nick could see them moving toward him. He keyed in the numbers. 5, 9, 3, 7, and 5, then pressed the red button. The clock above the numbers was still counting down.

"Zeke, it didn't work!"

Twenty seconds.

"It was right, I'm telling you, those are the numbers!" Zeke was shouting now. "Do it again, but this time press the red button twice!"

"Wait!" Nick shouted. The men were on top of him. "I'm Nick Campos! Ranger for the United States Army! Stand down!"

Fifteen seconds.

If it didn't work this time, he was going to have to run away from the White House as fast as he could and die with the blast.

He keyed again. 5, 9, 3, 7, and 5. This time he pressed the red button twice. The entire electronic face attached to the bomb began blinking red. Nick's eyes moved to the top of it. Thankfully, the countdown paused at ten seconds.

"Holy shit," one of the security guards said as he looked down over Nick. "You stopped it."

Nick let out a sigh of relief, but it was short lived. He looked up at the two security guards. "There's another bomb."

24

THE SECURITY GUARD SWALLOWED HIS FEAR AND GRABBED HIS radio. "We have a bomb. Go into full lockdown. I repeat, full lockdown!"

Nick was already on his feet talking to Zeke. "Where's the other bomb, Zeke? Did you see Nasir drop it?"

"A lot of things look the same back there, but yes. After he hit you, he ran straight for the backside of the house." Nick started jogging in that direction. "He passed the first bunch of flowers and stuff and went over to the ones in the middle."

Nick looked to his right before the security guards were out of sight and noticed that several military men had joined them. At least Nick didn't have to worry about friendly fire any longer—just a terrorist's bomb outside the White House. No biggie.

"Can you be more specific?" Nick moved past the first landscaped patch like Zeke had instructed. "'Cause this place is huge."

"I can't, really. I kept the ASE on Nasir. I can switch it back to you to try to help."

Nick could see now what Zeke meant by *the ones in the middle.* Up ahead, after a long break, there was another grouping of flowers and bushes. Nick ran forward.

"No, keep the ASE on Nasir. You shared it with Brooke, right?"

"Right. She texted and said she tried to call you. Hasn't found out what airport he flew into yet."

The first trickle of doubt that he'd be able to catch Nasir before he got away seeped into Nick's consciousness. It just couldn't happen. It would literally mean the difference in hundreds or even thousands of innocent lives before they could catch back up to him. Now that Nasir knew for certain that the frequency jammer would keep the ASE from locating him, he would surround himself with much larger versions of it. Nick knew after Brooke got up to speed with the ASE, she would get all hands on deck in locating the car. He just hoped it would be in time. She was good. Nick needed to trust that so he could focus.

Bottom line: they couldn't let Nasir get away. But the first order of business was disarming this last bomb. Zeke and Brooke had their eyes on Nasir. That would have to be good enough for now.

Nick was tearing through the landscaping that Zeke told him the bag was in. A lot of it was almost waist high, so the bag wasn't readily visible. That was undoubtedly the reason Nasir had dumped it here. Nick took a deep breath, in and out, and scanned the area slowly instead of trying to go so fast he'd miss seeing it.

"Zeke, just make sure that Brooke is getting law enforcement to ALL of the surrounding airports. I still can't find the bag."

Nick was looking left when his right foot kicked something solid. It was the bag. He dropped to his knees, opened the top, and found the bomb. He was relieved to see that there was thirteen minutes left on the timer. Nick figured the timers were preset, and Nasir didn't have time to make this one shorter. Thank god.

"Okay, Zeke, I've got the bag. What's the code?"

"What?" Zeke said.

"What do you mean what? The code! For the ticking bomb!"

There was hesitation. Nick's stomach dropped.

"Nick, I don't have the code for that one. I got lucky and saw all the numbers on the first one. Nasir typed in the code while he was running away after hitting you. There was no way I could zoom in in time to see it."

Nick wanted to say rewind it, but as of then, there was still no way to go back in time. Though the technology was amazing, it wasn't like the movies. You couldn't dial up a moment in time and rewatch. All you could do was record what you dialed up live, and if Zeke didn't see it live, he wouldn't see it in the replay.

Nick closed the bag and strapped it onto his back. He ended the call with Zeke and immediately dialed Brooke.

"Nick! You're all right!" Brooke answered.

"For now. Where's Nasir?"

Nick walked out of the landscaping. The military men were walking his way.

"I just got the ASE app Zeke sent me loaded to my phone, and got it running. I didn't know how to work it so it took a minute."

"Do you know where he is or not?"

Brooke paused. Nick didn't have time to worry about her feelings.

"Ummm . . . yes! He's already at an airport!"

"Shit. Which one?"

"The only one he could be at this quickly is Reagan," Brooke explained. "It's just a ten-minute drive from the White House."

"Get as many law enforcement personnel there as you can, I'm on my way!"

"Nick, you don't have to worry. They're already there. As soon as Zeke let me know what was happening, I dispatched law enforcement to all three airports and their private air divisions. We got a hit back on a private plane sitting at Signature at Reagan. It's the only plane that came in from international overnight. It has to be him! We're going to get him!"

Nick wanted to be happy, but he didn't believe it was going to be that easy. "Hold on, Brooke."

"I said, has the bomb been disabled?" the man shouted.

Nick's mind was racing.

Then Nick heard Brooke shouting through the phone." Nick! Can you hear me?"

"Hold on, guys," Nick said to security. When he turned his back to answer Brooke, the man grabbed his shoulder and spun him around. Nick pushed him back. "I said hold on!"

The two men raised their guns. "We need to see that bag, *now*!"

"Brooke, I have to go. I have a situation here."

"Nick! I just got word there was an ambush outside of the private plane. Law enforcement there is down."

"Down?" Nick could hardly hear her over the men shouting at him to drop the bag.

"Nasir had men waiting at the private airport in case

there was trouble. The receptionist called 911. Nick, she said they're all dead. All the police that was there! We're close ourselves, but there's no way we can beat him to the plane."

The men moved toward Nick, and he backpedaled quickly.

"Brooke, do not go near him! They'll kill you!"

The security guys were through waiting on Nick. One surged forward and grabbed his arm. Nick managed to rip his arm away, but the second man pointed his gun straight at Nick's chest. Finally, Nick raised his hands above his head. "All right! Relax, guys! The bomb has been disabled. Damn!" He had to lie to stall.

"Give us the bag or we'll take it."

Nick had known better than to think Nasir wouldn't have plans in case something went wrong. Now he had a clear lane out of the country. There was no one left to stop him, and no way for Nick to get to the airport in time *and* dispose of the bomb.

That was when he remembered the fob in his pocket. The first button—the cloaking device—was no help. But button number two was the only thing left that gave him the slight chance of stopping Nasir. He knew he was going to pay for it, but he didn't have a choice. He reached into his pocket and took the fob in his hand. As the two men rushed him and knocked him off his feet, he pressed down on button number two for dear life, counting to three in his head while the men were ripping the bomb bag away from him and tearing at his hand that clutched the fob.

Out of the corner of his eye, just before the big man hit him in the jaw, he noticed the light on the top of the fob flash green.

That green light meant that something Nick would have

laughed at a year ago, or called someone a child for believing in, was actually coming to help save a lot of lives. It meant that the sleigh pulled by eight majestic reindeer was on its way, and it meant he still had a shot at catching up to Nasir.

25

ONE OF THE MEN FINALLY WRESTLED THE FOB FROM NICK'S hand, as the other opened the bomb bag.

"Joe, this thing's still ticking down. It says there's only six minutes left!"

Nick squirmed away when the man on top of him was distracted and popped up to his feet. Behind the men, a dozen more uniformed soldiers were running his way, along with one guy in a suit.

"Put your hands behind your head, now!" The man with the fob extended his pistol with his right hand.

Nick did as he asked.

"If you know how to shut this thing off, you've gotta do it!"

Nick was calm. "If I knew, it would already be disabled."

The other men made it to where Nick was being held at gunpoint. The man holding the bomb shouted, "We need the bomb squad! We only have about five minutes!"

"You're Nick, right?" The man in the suit stepped forward, out of breath from his run.

"Yes. You have to let me have the bomb back. I can get rid of it."

"I can't let you have the bomb, Nick." Then to the man holding the gun on Nick, "But you can put the gun down, soldier. He's on our side."

The man began to lower the gun.

"I don't know who you are, but I'm taking the bag," Nick said. "It's the only way to keep all of us from getting killed."

The man in the suit was about to protest when Nick watched his eyes jump to the sky behind him. He could tell by the look on his face that the reindeer had just come into view. Nick was relieved to know they were about to land. All the men that were gathered around him lost track of everything but the unbelievable thing coming their way from the sky. Every single one of them watched as the reindeer landed on the south lawn of the White House. When Zeke disabled the cloaking device, it must have killed the one on the sleigh as well. And it might have just saved the day.

Nick turned to look as the reindeer and the sleigh glided onto the grass. The bells were jingling, and their hooves were pounding the ground until they came to a stop. Nick used the moment of shock to make his escape.

"Sorry, boys," he said. Then he ripped the fob from the hand of the man in front of him. He followed that with a hard right cross to the man's jaw that was holding the bag, and then he ripped it away from him. Before the stun of the situation could wear off, Nick was hopping up into the sleigh, and slapping the reins. "I've got a terrorist to catch. Ho ho ho!" He just couldn't help himself.

The sleigh started forward. Nick looked off to his right —toward the street. There were at least a dozen people with their cell phones out, recording the first actual footage of Santa's reindeer pulling a sleigh. There was nothing Nick could do about it, except apologize to them internally for the absence of presents under the tree tomorrow morning. Though he couldn't help but think that having a president that was still breathing was surely present enough.

The sleigh sped forward and lifted off the ground. A real show for the onlookers and their Facebook followers. But that was already out of Nick's mind. He glanced over at the bag and saw the red numbers ticking down. Only two minutes and forty-nine seconds to go. His first thought was to warp to the middle of nowhere and drop the bomb safely to the uninhabited ground below. But something down in his lizard brain was telling him there was no time, and that maybe, just maybe, the bomb could be of some use. He didn't know if it was his combat instinct—honed over countless missions into enemy territory––that was speaking to him, or just a ridiculous bit of bravado that made him think he could do it all. Either way, he was listening to it, and he gave the command for the Signature private aviation section of the Reagan International Airport. Nick texted Brooke, telling her he was on his way.

The reindeer responded, and the torque of their pull on the sleigh snapped Nick's neck back. The cold wind was blowing all around him as he used the short trip to start to devise a plan. He checked his belt. All he had there was a combat knife and his Beretta. Not nearly enough to thwart any sort of pushback he might have when he arrived He looked back over his shoulder and there sat the sack. The same one that had blown his mind when he'd discovered this crashed sleigh in the desert. A sack without a bottom was a hell of a thing. But when Jack showed him what it could really do, he knew one day it would be a life and death game changer.

Today was that day.

As the sleigh had already begun its descent, Nick turned and fished down into the sack. The way Jack had explained it was that it was like reaching into your closet. Whatever had been inventoried through the sack's *wormhole software*, as Jack had put it, would be available in the bag, wherever in the world you were. All you had to do was picture it, then reach in the sack, and pull it out. To Jack's chagrin, but Zeke's delight, the first thing Nick had inventoried were the guns Zeke had procured for him. An entire closet full.

Nick closed his eyes and pictured the M-60 that sat at the very back of his gun closet in the warehouse. He reached down into the sack, and sure enough, his hand wrapped around the feeder tray. Pulling magic out of the sack never got old. He hoisted the large, belt-fed, fully automatic machine gun from the sack and pulled it over into the front seat beside him. The M-60 had mostly been replaced in actual combat, but Nick had a fondness for it that had lasted since he first held one in his hands over two decades ago.

Nick checked the bomb—only a minute and thirty-two seconds to go. While Nick didn't know a lot about Reagan International, he did know that the runway was right next to the Potomac River. Worst case scenario, he would fly right over it and dump the bomb into the water at the last second. He just hoped he could take out Nasir before then.

26

As THE GROUND WAS GETTING CLOSER BENEATH HIM, HE turned back around for the sack. This time, he pictured the disintegrating hundred-cartridge belt that fed the machine gun and pulled it out as well. The reindeer were leveling out, ready to land at the private side of the massive airport. Nick didn't hear any gunshots coming from below, but he didn't know if that was good or bad. He took the M-60 in his hand, lined the cartridge belt up with the feed hole, pushed it in over the ridge, then pulled back the cocking lever and pushed it back forward. As the skis on the bottom of the sleigh slid atop the grass that sat beside the parking lot, the M-60 was loaded and ready to fire. Nick just hoped there would still be something to shoot at.

When he looked to his left, he saw Brooke sprinting out of the airport. "Nick! He's taking off! It's too late!"

Nick moved the M-60 over into his lap. "He hasn't left yet?"

"The jet is moving out onto the runway now."

"Then I still have time."

"You can't go out there. Can that gun even stop a plane like that?"

"We're about to find out. What's the tail number?"

"I—I can't remember. But it's black. The lady just said it's the only black one out there."

Nick whistled and used his right hand to slap the reins. "Were going after the black plane, boys and girls. I'm gonna need your best!"

Nick didn't know what, or if they really understood, but he felt like saying it out loud might help them.

Brooke took a step back. "Nick, don't! We'll find out where he's landing. Don't put all of these people in danger."

The sleigh edged forward.

"Where Nasir is going to land that plane, they don't have flight plans. No one will know where he is. More people than we can count will die if I don't get to him here."

The sleigh bolted forward.

Nick glanced back over his shoulder one last time. Brooke's face held worry. He could see that she really cared what happened to him.

"Be careful!" she shouted. He barely heard her, but he didn't need to. It was written all over her face.

Nick gave her a confident nod as the reindeer veered to the left, up and over the barrier to the airfield. *Careful* would have no part in the next sixty seconds. Which was all the time he had left before the bomb would blow him and the reindeer to the North Pole if he didn't get rid of it.

Nick obviously knew Reagan was a busy airport, but when they cleared the fence and got some height, the planes were like ants on an anthill. Fortunately, most were commercial airliners—much bigger than the private plane Nasir would be on. And now that he was closer, it was even more helpful that it was black. While there was a lot of traffic on the runways, Nick knew Nasir's pilot would not be waiting patiently in line like everyone else.

This would cause multiple problems for Nick. One: He had to be very careful about where exactly he steered the sleigh. If he got too far out over the runways, he could easily be hit by a plane taking off or landing. Two: If he started shooting his M-60 as the reindeer were flying, the bullets could go anywhere. And those spent rounds could easily skip into a nearby plane and either kill a passenger or hit something and blow an entire plane. Those were risks Nick was not willing to take. However, there was also the matter of the ticking bomb. Time to do *anything* was running short.

Nick looked down to his left, then steered the reindeer over and looked to his right. He was in dangerous territory now––planes were everywhere. But that was when he spotted a black jet taxiing quickly to the first large runway. Nick tugged on the reins, making the reindeer loop the sleigh out to the right, and then down. Nasir's jet was going to be on his left. He let go of the reins and took the M-60 in his hands. He scooted to the edge of the sleigh and placed the butt of the gun to his shoulder.

As the sleigh made a pass, Nick wrapped his finger around the trigger. An unexpected flame of anger sparked inside him. As they came around the backside of the plane, the image of his closest friend, Ricky "Gunner" Thompson, flashed in his mind. His crooked smile, bowlegged walk, and gut-busting laugh all played like a movie in front of the terrorist's escape vehicle. Nick could feel the emotion rising. That was when the final scene of his friend's life rolled. It was like Nick was back in the desert. They had been taking fire from all angles. Nick had been trying to cover the remaining members of his team, when an explosion erupted up on his right. Nick remembered watching as

Jimmy's body disintegrated in front of him. A leg had bounced left, and an arm had catapulted forward. His closest friend had just been blown to smithereens. All because of the monster riding in the black jet that was now squarely in Nick's sights. Nick and his team had been there to support another team that had become trapped. They'd ended up in a fire sack, over half of his men––dead. Including Ricky.

Nick cleared the nightmare from his head. When he focused in on the plane, he was in perfect position to fire.

So he did.

Tat tat tat tat tat tat tat!

A string of rounds exploded out of the M-60, and rocketed toward the black jet, but Nick wouldn't see if they hit. He was too busy being thrown into the floor of the sleigh. When the loud bangs from his machine gun popped off, the reindeer jerked right and toward the sky. The thought that he might frighten them never even crossed Nick's mind. He was used to shooting from tanks, not from behind animals. And their reaction—though obvious in hindsight—caught Nick entirely by surprise.

When he fell on his back, the M-60 ripped from his hands and clanked off the seat behind him. It then ricocheted off the rail and down over the side. Nick pulled himself to a seated position, but the G-force of the reindeer pulling away in fear wouldn't allow him to grab the reins. All he could do was hold on. When they shifted course left, then back to the right, Nick watched the bomb bag begin to slide down the seat. He didn't panic often, but if that bag fell down to the runway, it would be a bigger disaster than if he had just left it sitting outside the White House. And he couldn't let that happen.

27

LOSING THE MACHINE GUN WAS BAD. NICK HAD A LOT OF weapons in his inventory, but none of them would do the damage the M-60 could do—which was enough damage to bring down a plane. He didn't know exactly what he could do with the bomb in the backpack, but he knew it was the only chance he had left to make sure Nasir didn't get away.

"Whoa!" Nick shouted. "Whoa, reindeer!" The bag slid again. This time, he could tell it was going to go the distance and slide right out of the sleigh.

Nick pivoted on the balls of his feet, let go of his grip on the seat and the front rail, and dove for the bag. The bag banged against the inside of the sleigh, fell onto the floor, and disappeared over the side. Nick shot his hand down as he rammed into the side of the sleigh, and he was just able to catch the top strap on the bag. Nick slid his body out over the edge and saw that the bag had landed on the ski beneath him. It had been the only reason he'd been lucky enough to get a grip on it before it fell to the planes below.

The reindeer leveled out, and Nick was able to pull himself back up and inside. As he grabbed the reins with his left hand and pulled, he flipped open the top flap of the bag.

Thirty seconds.

It was decision time. Fly over the Potomac and drop the bag in, *or* take one last pass at Nasir. Nick was able to slow the reindeer and pull them back around. Nasir's pilot had been able to worm his way around to the head of the runway. He was about to take off. As Nick pulled the sleigh around so he was coming up behind Nasir's jet, he wondered if there was any more magic in Santa's ride. Because if he was going to attempt the idea that just popped into his mind, he was going to need a little help from the fat guy, or at least from *someone* looking down on him from the other realm. Nick glanced at the bomb.

Twenty-five seconds.

It was crazy. He looked out over the reindeer. Though he knew they were afraid, they were still willing to go––moving immediately when he tugged the reins. As he stared down the back of the jet, watching it begin to move down the runway, he realized he had to take a shot. The runway was clear in front of the black jet, and no one was behind them now. It was clear that the tower had advised the other planes to keep their distance from the black one that had been steering crazily across the tarmac.

Nick slapped the reins, and the brave reindeer surged forward. "Give me all you've got!"

They did. The sleigh shot forward, pinning Nick to the back of his seat. He took the bomb bag in his right hand and slid over to the far left side of the sleigh. When Jack had taught Nick how to "drive" the sleigh, he talked about how the reindeer could hear him if his mind was quiet. He could help direct them without speaking a command. Nick had thought at first that, like everything else about the North

Pole, this had to be total bullshit. But now he was quiet. Now that Nick was intensely focused on the monster in that plane in front of them, the reindeer slid in position as if Nick was guiding them by hand.

Nice and steady. Just get me as close to that plane as you can.

The black jet was really moving now--rocketing down the middle of the runway. Nick glanced over at the bag.

Fifteen seconds.

Nick didn't know a lot about planes. He was Army, not Air Force. But he did know that the plane was getting ready to leave the runway. It was go time.

Give me a little of that warp, guys, he directed a thought to the reindeer.

When the sleigh pulled forward, he couldn't believe it. But he didn't dwell on it. Instead, he tightened his grip on the bag and focused on the right wing of the jet. He had one shot at this before Nasir would be able to fly away--maybe this time, disappearing forever.

The tips of this particular jet's wings weren't like a commercial aircraft. Instead of just smoothly coming to a point, the tips of the wings on this plane curved up a foot or two into the air at the ends and narrowed to a thin point at the top. Nick assumed it was for aerodynamics. But for his purposes, it was there to hold a special gift.

The plane's wheels began to lift off the ground. The reindeer avoided the jet wash by staying outside the wing as the sleigh pulled even. *Get me a little closer,* he thought. The plane's nose tilted skyward. Nick couldn't believe it, but not only did the reindeer pull him closer, they also tilted up, matching the trajectory of the jet. Nick saw the runway turn into water below as they moved out over the river. The bomb was still ticking down.

Ten seconds.

Nick leaned out over the edge. He hooked his right elbow around the end of the front rail and leaned out. He held the back strap of the bag in a death grip with his left hand and extended his arm outward. The tip of the wing was right there. He just needed a little bit more. The pull of the wind against the bag was insane, and the strap was slipping from his fingers. His arms were on fire.

Closer, he thought.

The sleigh inched closer at his plea. He extended as far as his right arm would let him, but he needed a little more to hook the bag. The reindeer understood without him having to ask. As the pull of the wind became too much for Nick, he shot his left arm forward with all the power he had left. Just as the plane moved away from the sleigh on a new heading, Nick let go of the strap, and it caught on the upward tip of the wing, then slid down and pinned itself, trapping it to the plane.

Nick slid over to the middle of the seat and took hold of the reins. Slowly pulling back, letting the reindeer know they had done their job. He watched as the black jet moved away from them in the deep blue sky. As it did, Nick counted down in his head.

Three . . . Two . . . One . . .

Subconsciously, a smile grew across Nick's face. "Merry Christmas motherfu--"

BOOM!

Nick had seen a lot of explosions over the years, but none had been more beautiful than this. The ball of fire plumed in the distance against the deep blue sky. The man who'd taken far too many innocent people to their graves would never see one of his own. There was a special place in hell for people like Nasir Samara, and Nick was just happy to be the one to be able to put him where he belongs.

Nick took a long, deep breath as he took it all in. His heart was pounding, and his adrenaline was pumping. He'd done it. He got the bastard that killed his brothers-in-arms —the same son of a bitch that had murdered his friend.

"For you, Ricky. RIP, brother."

Nick slapped the reins against the rail, and once again told the reindeer, "Take me home."

28

A FROZEN WIND BLEW THROUGH THE STREETS OF THE NORTH Pole. With it came snowflakes. They danced and swayed toward the ground, aglow in all the colors from the lights that lined every single house in the village. Every Christmas Eve night at the North Pole had always been a frenzy. Elves were always running on weary legs to get the last of the presents properly inventoried, so Santa would be able to pluck just the right gift, for just the right little boy or girl, at just the right house.

There was a frenzy this Christmas Eve night as well, but it wasn't like those of the past. This time, instead of putting the finishing touches on the celebration feast set for Christmas Day, Mrs. Claus was leading all the elves in the village in a march toward Nick's front door.

Inside Nick's house, he'd just got the fire going in the living room. He stabbed at the logs being singed by the yellow-orange flame with his wrought-iron poker, then placed it back in the stand when the wood began to pop and crack. One of his favorite sounds. He shuffled over to the recliner that he'd pushed to the middle of the room—the fireplace at his feet—and his sixty-five-inch flat-panel TV hanging perfectly above the mantle. He switched it on, flipped over to ESPN, and to the only bowl game that was on that evening. It was the Hawaii Bowl. Nick didn't have a clue who was playing, nor did he care.

He reached over to the table he'd pulled over beside the chair, picked up the bottle of Woodford Reserve Double Oaked bourbon, and poured enough in his glass to kill the aching in his shoulder from smacking into the side of the sleigh no more than an hour ago. Before he took a drink, he picked up his cutter and snipped the end of his Cuban Cohiba Robusto. He then struck a match, held the flame to the end of his cigar, and turned it clockwise in his fingers while he puffed to get a perfect, even burn. The cigar had a slightly salty taste that paired exquisitely with the sweet bourbon he sipped as the smoke plumed in the air.

After another drink, the weight of the last two days finally began to pull him down. He was tired. It had been a long time since he'd been in any sort of combat situation. It was clear he needed to step up his training if he was going to continue this whole Saint Nick gig. The satisfaction of seeing Nasir's plane explode was enough to make him want to do it more. However, at the moment, he was content to be left to his vices. He felt he deserved some time to revel in the day's accomplishment.

When he arrived back at the NP, he'd been greeted by a mob of worried and angry little elves. He told them all to go back to bed, because he had already delivered the only present he was going to deliver that Christmas. They of course had no idea what he meant, but they didn't need to know the details of taking down one of the world's scariest monsters. He'd seen the hurt in Jack's eyes, and Mrs. Claus —though happy he was back safe—couldn't hide her disappointment that Christmas was canceled this year.

Nick had tried to thank Jack for his lesson on how to steer the reindeer with his mind. He'd told him it saved his life, and probably a lot of others, but not even that was enough to bring Jack out of his sorrow. Nick never had been into the Christmas holiday, but he imagined that even if he had, he still wouldn't care enough to ride back out into the world to dispense toys. Not on that evening anyway. Zeke had been the only one there that had actually been happy to see Nick after he announced he wasn't delivering presents. But after a quick thank you for helping save the president's life, and his own back at the White House, he sent Zeke home. He was too tired to entertain.

Nick had sent the sleigh back down to DC to pick up Brooke. If she even wanted to come to the North Pole. He didn't actually know where she stood with things now that Nasir was gone and Agent Andrews, who had assigned her to Nick, was dead. He figured she would probably just want to go home. He couldn't blame her for that. Though, there was a part of him that had hoped she might be ringing his doorbell. He didn't really know why he felt that way. He knew that Brooke hated him. That was probably why he'd started to like her—he always had taken the hardest route in life.

Any way he looked at it—the village being mad at him, Brooke not wanting to see him, and kids not getting presents that night—he didn't really care. He had his bourbon, his cigar, a nice warm bed to finally get some rest in, and that was enough for him.

Ding dong. The doorbell rang.

Nick took another sip of bourbon, turned the volume

up on the TV, and took another puff. The smells of wood burning, sweet cigar smoke, and whiskey intoxicated his senses enough to not give a damn who was at the front door.

Ding dong. Ding dong.

Nick placed his cigar on the ashtray and checked his phone. No messages from Brooke. So again—about the front door—he didn't care. Hawaii just scored a touchdown on the screen. Number eighty-four made a hell of a one-handed catch. The announcer was losing his mind. Nick rolled his eyes. It was just a C-level bowl game that had absolutely no meaning. The dude was going wild like it was the National Championship.

Ding dong-ding dong-ding dong!

"All right! I hear you! Good god. Can't a guy get a break?" Nick shouted. He muted the barking announcer, swallowed the rest of his bourbon, and limped over to the window. When he pulled back the curtain, he couldn't see who was actually ringing the doorbell, but he could see that the mass of elves had flocked to his doorstep. He felt like they might be ready to burn him at the stake.

Nick's phone started to ring. He walked back over to the table—it was Brooke.

"Hello?"

"Answer the front door, would you?" Brooke said.

"Why? So they can tell me how I ruined Christmas? I'm not in the mood."

"Just open the door. I'm the only one coming in."

"Fine," he said with a sigh.

Nick poured another Woodford and sipped it on the way to the door. The cold air rushed in, but it wasn't enough to cool the warm feeling that moved through him when he saw Brooke standing there. Of course he knew she was going to be there, but he hadn't expected her to look like that.

"Aren't you going to invite me in? It's not exactly balmy out here."

"Oh—yes. Sorry. I just . . ." Nick didn't know what he meant to say. He'd never seen Brooke the way he did when she was standing under that yellow light. Her skin was glowing beneath her long blonde hair. The fluffy white lapel of the red coat she had on was stunning on her. *She* was stunning.

"You all right, Nick?"

He closed the door behind her. He was trying to find words, but a woman hadn't stolen his breath in so long that it was taking him a minute to catch up.

"Do you mind?" she said. She was holding the lapels of her coat out. It took Nick a second.

"Huh? Oh, yes. Sorry." He reached for the collar and pulled it off of her. The red turtleneck beneath the coat hugged her figure. Also something Nick hadn't noticed until now. Before he could say anything, both of them heard something outside.

Brooke walked over to the window to have a look. "Doesn't sound like they want to tell you that you've ruined Christmas to me."

Nick dialed into the elves and their chant.

Santa. Santa. Santa. Santa.

Brooke walked past him into the living room and warmed her hands by the fire. Then she looked back over her shoulder. Nick wasn't sure, but she looked disappointed.

Nick followed her into the room and took a sip of his drink. "What? I'm not Santa, Brooke. I don't know what they want from me."

She stopped warming her hands and put them on her hips. "I don't understand you, Nick."

"Welcome to the club."

"No, don't do that." She walked over to him. Right in his face now. "Don't play into the persona that you're this macho guy who doesn't give a damn. 'Cause I know it's bullshit."

Nick furrowed his brow. "You don't even know me. How would you know if it's a persona, or if it's just who I am?"

Brooke reached out and grabbed his hand. He almost recoiled, but left it instead. "Because I saw who you were today, Nick. You can't hide behind the *I'm the grizzled, and aloof* guy that doesn't care what happens to people. Not after you risked your life on a number of occasions—just today—for people you don't even know. Just so strangers can be safe and enjoy the freedoms that guys like you fight for all the time. You are the exact opposite of the man you're claiming to be, and I don't understand why. It's a beautiful thing."

This was all getting awkward for Nick. He'd never had someone—not since his grandmother—praise him in any sort of way. All he was used to was getting cursed out by the commanding officer. A hard man who only told him how miserable and useless he was. The same way his mother had before she left. He just wanted to change the subject.

"What does this have to do with delivering presents to a bunch of spoiled brats? Playing Santa is a lot different than saving lives, Brooke."

"No, Nick. It's not."

"Where'd you get that outfit anyway?" He'd have preferred to talk about *anything* else.

"When I got back here, I went to see Mrs. Claus first. I

had a nice long conversation with her. She gave me this to wear. What of it?"

"So that's what took you so long." Nick knew he shouldn't have said it as soon as it left his mouth.

Brooke smiled. He wasn't sure, but he also thought maybe her eyes were sparkling. The bourbon must have been kicking in.

"What's that? Mr. I Don't Care wasn't worried about me, was he?"

She held her smile as she snatched his glass, downed what was left, then handed him back the empty glass.

"I'm not saying you're a gentleman, Nick. Hell, you didn't even offer me a drink. What I'm saying is that after talking to Mrs. Claus, you and *Santa* actually have a lot in common."

Nick walked over to the kitchen, grabbed a second glass, and walked back to the bourbon. He spoke as he poured. "Like what, Brooke? The fact that we are both men? That's about the only comparison I can draw. You're not seriously equating what I do by putting my life on the line every day to dropping presents down a chimney are you?"

The chants outside were getting louder. *We want Nick! We want Nick! We want Nick!*

Brooke ignored them to answer Nick's question. "I am, actually."

Nick scoffed as he walked over to her and handed her a drink.

"Can I talk without you making noises at me?" she said.

Nick took a step back and motioned with his hand for her to go on.

"I actually do think they are comparable. I'm not saying that one is more important than the other, I'm simply saying they both are. Because they both help to make the world a better place. Everyone is different, Nick. Not everyone possesses that same set of skills. You have to use what you are good at to make a difference. *That* is how you are the same."

Brooke stepped forward and placed her hand on his arm. "Nick, what both of you do is you give people hope. When you rid the planet of a man that does terrible things to our world, you give people something to believe in. When they see what you do, it inspires them. It makes them understand that someone is out there fighting for them. And it makes them want to fight, too. And what Santa has always done, Nick, is show people that there is kindness in the world. That not all people are like the bad people that you fight every day. Santa shows them that doing things for other people—*loving* other people—that makes the world a better place too. And as silly as you think spending your life giving kids toys might be, it might just be the only toy they *ever* receive. Not everyone is spoiled. Far from it. And that kind gesture might just keep that child from turning into someone that you have to save the world from later in life. Can you understand that at all? It's important, too."

Nick stared at the fire and took another drink. He wasn't used to all these . . . *feelings.*

We want Nick! We want Nick! We want Nick!

"You know, I didn't ask for any of this," Nick said.

"Neither did I, Nick. But I'm still here."

The front door burst open, and Zeke came running in. He was holding the Iron Man Santa suit from the warehouse. He stopped at the entrance to the living room and held up the suit, proud as he could be.

Nick picked up the bottle of bourbon. "Fine. I'll deliver the stupid presents."

Brooke and Zeke both smiled and pumped their fists.

Nick walked around the chair and looked at Brooke. "But I'm not going alone. You're coming with me."

Brooke smiled and hooked her arm around his. "As long as you bring that bottle, I'm in," she said with a wink.

Nick looked over at Zeke and shook his head.

"All right, let's go . . . But . . . I am *not* wearing that stupid suit."

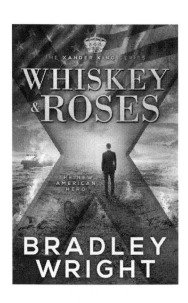

The Xander King Series
by
Bradley Wright

———————————————

WHISKEY & ROSES: Imagine James Bond meets Mitch Rapp.

———————————————

The world knows him as a handsome, charismatic, and successful young businessman. The CIA knows Xander as the US military's most legendary soldier, turned vigilante assassin, who sharpens his skills in the shadows until he can exact revenge on the monster who murdered his family. They have watched his double life go on long enough, and now the government wants their weapon back.

SAMPLE: WHISKEY & ROSES

Chapter 1: The Legend of Xander King

"Some people don't deserve to live. One man is *exceptional* at making sure they don't," Director William Manning announced as he addressed the roomful of the CIA's finest. "The decision that lies before us is whether we make this man an ally or an enemy. And I'm afraid we can't afford the latter."

Just before Director Manning blasted into the room and uttered those chilling words, Sarah Gilbright sat alone trying desperately to keep from nervous-sweating through her blouse. She knew it wasn't all that unusual for the director of the CIA to call a top secret meeting of the seven highest-ranking officials in the agency. However, it was highly unusual for the eighth person involved in that meeting to be a comparatively low-ranked special agent like herself. Sarah knew there could only be one reason she had been invited to a meeting so far above her clearance level: they had decided to do something about Xander King.

Sarah fidgeted in her seat and shuffled through her prepared portfolios. She felt as if she were back in college. The plain white walls of the square room, the cheap collapsible faux-wood tables, and the metal folding chairs were almost enough to give her that familiar college hungover feeling.

That was when the heavy wooden door flung open,

clanging against the painted cinder block wall with a loud crash, and Director Manning buzzed into the room. Though he didn't look anything like the TV character, his clumsy, hurried entry reminded Sarah of Kramer from *Seinfeld*. No, Director Manning couldn't have looked less like Cosmo Kramer. Manning's short, stout frame and his cloud-white hair made certain of that.

Director Manning finished his morbid opening remarks about Xander.

"Either way, enemy or ally, we've got to do something. Let's get through this as quickly as possible." His tone was more of a growl as he dropped his black leather briefcase onto the table. The button on his light-gray suit jacket seemed to be holding on by a mere thread.

Sarah imagined the button on his pants probably shared a similar stretch.

"All of you know each other, with the exception of Special Agent Sarah Gilbright here." Manning pointed to Sarah.

The palms of Sarah's hands filled with sweat at the sound of her name among all those important people. This was a big damn deal. She played it off as best she could, tucking her long blonde hair back behind her ear.

"Sarah, if you could please hand everyone a file and come up front with me."

She did as Manning asked and began passing around Xander's file. She worried that her slim-fitting black skirt and tight royal-blue silk blouse might be inappropriate. She had decided to button one more button on her blouse in the bathroom just moments ago. It was hard for her to contain her mother's gift of large breasts, but she wanted the men in this meeting to take her seriously. The women too. She wanted them all to listen because of her merit, not because of her curves and slender waist, as had all too often been the case since she joined the agency.

Director Manning continued. "Six months ago I gave Sarah an assignment to keep an eye on a man named Alexander King. I'm sure that all of you have heard the name at one time or another due to the legend of his time in our military, but his service to our country has taken on a much different role these days. Sarah is going to fill us in, and then we are going to figure out just what in the hell we are going to do about him. Sarah?"

Sarah handed off her last file and took the podium in front of the deputy and executive directors, the head of admin, the head of espionage, and the head of public affairs for the Central *freaking* Intelligence Agency of the United States of *freaking* America.

Wow.

Her voice was shaky. "Good afternoon, everyone. It's an honor to—"

"Sarah . . . all due respect, spare us," Director Manning broke in. "We have other things to worry about so please keep this short."

"Yes, sir, Mr. Manning. Alexander King." She did as she was told and got right to it, swallowing the growing nerves and digging in. "All of you are familiar with the name?"

The roomful of stuffy higher-ups all nodded in unison.

Sarah continued. "The Alexander—Xander—King of today is known to the world as the billionaire son of Martin King, of King Oil. After his parents were brutally murdered in front of him, Xander decided not to follow in his father's footsteps. Instead, he sold King Oil and, as you well know by his *legend*, as Director Manning put it, he joined the navy. If you will, please open to the first page of the portfolio."

"And he's handsome," Mary Hartsfield, Director of Espionage, remarked when she opened the folder and saw a picture of Xander holding a bottle of bourbon.

"Mary, please. Could you wait till you get the portfolio home before you start drooling over it?" Director Manning scolded.

The group laughed at Mary's outburst, and Sarah, for the first time since entering the room, let the tension fall from her shoulders. She looked again, for probably the thousandth time, at the blue eyes staring at her in that picture and wholeheartedly agreed with Mary.

"I'm with you, Mary, he is quite handsome."

Director Manning rolled his eyes and motioned for Sarah to move on.

"That bottle in his hand is from his own bourbon company—King's Ransom—that he launched recently, and as some of you may or may not have heard, he has a horse by the same name running in the Kentucky Derby this coming Saturday. Those are the things he's known for to the outside world. However, the reason we are here today is because of what the public doesn't know, what Xander King doesn't know we know, and the reason Director Manning has had me monitoring Xander for the last six months. Xander King is an *assassin*."

The air in the room changed, shifting with the dark word Sarah uttered, surprising them all.

"Now, before you get the wrong idea about Xander, let me brief you on exactly what I mean."

Sarah turned the page, and the picture this time was of a beautiful dark-haired woman whose stern demeanor suggested she had seen her share of cruelty in the world.

"If you'll turn the page, you'll find Samantha Harrison, or Sam, as Xander calls her. Sam had quite the reputation at MI6 in the UK for being what used to be an unparalleled agent. We aren't exactly sure how she and Xander initially connected, but together they have formed quite a team. Sam is in charge of finding and coordinating the targets, and Xander goes about eliminating them. She is the coach, and he is the talent, if you will."

"Targets, Ms. Gilbright?" Mary asked.

"Yes, targets. The scum of the earth. The most evil and vile human beings on the planet."

Deputy Director Richards, a silver-haired, tall, and lanky man, spoke up. "And he just kills them? No justice system? Vigilante style, he's the judge and jury? I see now why we are here. This is a problem."

Sarah felt the mood in the room shift again, and she wanted to make sure she gave the rest of the facts in such a manner to show that what Xander was doing, though not legal, was just about the most noble and honorable thing a man with his particular set of skills could do. She had been watching him for months. All of the charity events he had hosted, all of the people he had saved by taking out these miserable targets. She didn't want this audience to get the wrong impression of him.

"Well, I understand your skepticism, Mr. Richards, but I assure you this isn't some amateur running around killing random people he thinks *might* be doing bad things. Sam painstakingly researches each and every target, and if you will turn the page, I'll introduce you to some of these evil people."

They all turned the page. There was a picture of a forty-something man with an emptiness to his stare.

"The first man you see was killed by Xander three months ago. Jerrold Connors. Jerrold was—"

"Hey, I remember this guy," Deputy Director Richards interjected. "We were building a case against him when he was suddenly killed. Horrible, the things he was doing. Didn't we find the bodies of more than seven male teenagers out in his shed?"

"Yes, that's the guy."

"Awful. I remember, they were all drugged and tortured over a span of months, if I'm not mistaken."

"You are not mistaken. I'm glad you remember, Mr. Richards."

Director Manning cleared his throat. "Move along, Sarah."

"Right. The second target on the list, Mitch Boyle, was eliminated last month—"

"Oh God." Mary winced. "I remember him. He was the guy—the nurse—who was going around stealing newborn babies from the hospital nursery, then taking them home, killing them, and stuffing them like dolls."

"Good God," the Head of Public Affairs blurted.

Sarah could already feel that they were coming to understand Xander like she did. She had been skeptical at first too. She had thought there was no way this could be right, a man exacting vigilante justice; then she spent time getting to know him from afar. "I know. It's terrible. Mitch Boyle was a monster."

Director Manning cut in again. "Look, I think we get the point. The other six *monsters* on this page all deserve what Xander gave them, but that isn't what we need to focus on. Get to that please, Sarah."

Director Manning paused, then held up his hand. "You know what, actually . . . let me just take it from here." He stood up and shuffled Sarah to the side.

"But Director Manning—"

"Thank you, Sarah," he said, dismissing her. Sarah took a seat by the podium. She wanted to give them a better sense of things. She wasn't sure they understood Xander yet. She didn't want them to stop the good things he was doing to right the wrongs the judicial system couldn't manage to take care of. There was nothing more she could do now, though; it was Manning's show. She had assumed he was thinking the same way she was, but he had called this meeting for a reason.

Manning took the podium. "Now, the way I see it, we have three options here. One, we could shut Xander down and bring him up on charges . . ."

Sarah's stomach dropped.

"Two, we could let Mr. King continue to go about this, what I think we all would agree is noble work and just continue to monitor him—"

"What, and just let him play like he's Batman?" Richards interjected.

"Deputy Richards, I understand that concern, and that's why I think my third option is the only way to go. We will just have to be careful how we go about it."

"Which is?" Richards said.

"Which is, we get him to go to work for us."

Sarah tried to hold her tongue, but she couldn't. "Xander will never work for the government, Director Manning. You're wasting your time on that notion."

"Now hold on, Sarah. I just told you we would have to be careful how we went about it."

"I don't understand, why wouldn't we just *make* him work for us?" Mary asked. "We do have evidence that he has killed these people."

Again Sarah couldn't help herself. "He just simply won't do it—"

Director Manning gave Sarah an "I'm warning you" glare and continued to explain. "What Ms. Gilbright is so passionately stating is that Xander doesn't agree with how the United States government goes about some of its business. He made this very clear when he abruptly left our Special Ops team. He loves his country, but not its governing body."

"Xander was Special Ops?" Mary said.

"Xander King was everything you could be in our military. After his parents died, his sole mission was revenge and he wanted to be trained by the best. He joined the navy, quickly becoming a Navy SEAL; then in record time he was running Special Ops missions. I'm not sure what you have or have not heard, but he just might be the best damn soldier this military has *ever* known."

"So what happened?" Mary asked.

"Well, like a lot of our soldiers, he didn't agree with the missions he was sent on and frankly, as you all know, some of the innocent casualties that go along with keeping this country safe. So he'd had enough. To be honest with you, I'm not so sure this wasn't his plan all along."

"What do you mean?" Richards asked.

"I mean, I think he used our military."

"Used us?"

"Don't get me wrong, he laid his life on the line every single day for his country, but yes, I think ultimately he used us. I think the only thing Xander ever wanted was to find the people responsible for the murder of his parents."

"And he used the military to train him to do so," Mary Hartsfield said as she let that sink in.

"That's right. But we *need* a man like this. A man with his skills. Sometimes a surgical strike works far better than bringing in the entire army. Saves a lot of lives too. As you know, things are getting downright scary on the terrorist front and we could use a silent weapon like King."

Mary stood up. "So what then? What are we supposed to do?"

"The only thing we can do. Use our resources to find what he wants before he finds it. Then we give it to him . . . at a price."

"We find out who killed his parents and force him to do jobs for us for the information." Richards recognized the direction Manning was suggesting.

"It's the only way it will work." Manning hiked up his pants. "He will go to prison before he stops hunting their killer, and we can't have that happen. We can't lose him. He wouldn't go to prison anyway; he has too many resources. If he really wanted to, he could just disappear. That is why we have to take our time and get this right, and that is why Sarah is going to head up a team that will monitor Xander and Sam while finding the information that King desires."

Sarah couldn't contain the joy she found in that news, and a smile grew across her face.

"When we find that information—who killed Xander's family—we will approach him. But . . ."

Manning paused and looked over to Sarah.

"We have to be careful. If something goes wrong, if Xander were to kill the wrong person and it gets out that we knew what he was doing and we let it happen, we kiss all of our jobs good-bye."

Richards stood and gathered his things. "If you don't mind me asking, sir, why take the risk? You ask me, we should shut him down and find a soldier who *wants* to work for us. There has to be a hundred guys in our great military who can do the jobs we need done, the jobs he can do—"

"I assure you there is not."

Director Manning's expression was dead serious.

"There isn't one. Not in our military, or any other military. That's the only reason I would even call this meeting. If it was someone besides King doing this, we *would* just shut it down. But this soldier is special. We just have to make him an offer he can't refuse, and we need to do it fast. As far as I'm concerned, this is of the highest priority. The United States needs Xander King."

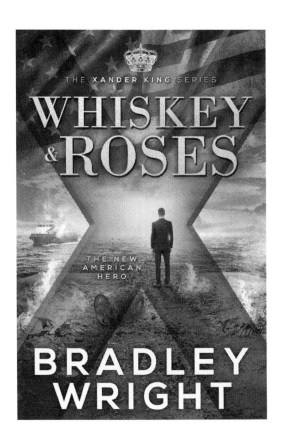

GET YOUR COPY TODAY
Only at Amazon.com
Free on Kindle Unlimited

ACKNOWLEDGMENTS

First and foremost, I want to thank you, the reader. I love what I do, and no matter how many people help me along the way, none of it would be possible if you weren't turning the pages.

To my family and friends. Every creative person is neurotic as hell about their creations, and I just want to thank you for always helping to keep my head on straight. And for indulging all of my ridiculous ideas.

To my editor, Josiah Davis. Thank you for continuing to turn my poorly constructed sentences into a readable story. You are great at what you do, and my work is better for it.

To my advanced reader team. You are my megaphone in helping spread the word about each new novel I release. You all have become friends, and I thank you for catching those last few sneaky typos, and always letting me know when something isn't good enough. Saint Nick appreciates you, and so do I.

ABOUT THE AUTHOR

Bradley Wright is the bestselling author of seven novels. He lives with his family in Lexington, Kentucky. He has always been a fan of great stories, whether it be a song, a movie, a novel, or a binge-worthy television series. Bradley loves interacting with readers on Facebook, Twitter, and via email.

Join the online family:
www.bradleywrightauthor.com
info@bradleywrightauthor.com

Made in the USA
Las Vegas, NV
17 December 2022